The Doctor

RED RIDGE CHRONICLES BOOK 4

SARAH LAMB

Contents

To each of the special people who have helped me bring this series and many of my other books to life: Brooke, for her on-point suggestions and proofreading; Nancy, for her fantastic covers; Spencer, for his incredible narration; and you, dear readers, for your endless support. It takes a village, and I'd be lost without mine.

***

And, thank you to each of you who voted if Hannah and Eli's baby should be a boy or a girl. You surprised me, as I didn't think that would be the one chosen!

Chapter 1

1870s, Red Ridge, Oregon

The stage slowed, and dust billowed around them. Nora pressed her handkerchief to her nose and squinted to protect her eyes. Almost every inch of her was covered in dust, and she longed for a proper bath, clean clothes, and a chance to stretch her legs. It was good to finally be in Red Ridge.

She had practically been sitting on the edge of her seat for the past hour. It had been too long since she had last visited.

To make matters worse, she'd left right in the middle of all of the excitement with Billy and the girl he liked, Mirabelle. It had nearly eaten her alive, wanting to know what had happened, until his letter arrived saying all was well.

The too-short trip to Red Ridge last time had filled Nora with a burning desire to return. Not just to spend time with Billy, and see that he and Mirabelle were well with her own eyes, but because she had the strangest feeling something else was about to happen, and she wanted to be there. Luckily, this time, she was there for an extended stay.

It was nice to get away for a while. This would also be a well-deserved break. With her father ready to retire, her assistance was no longer needed at home or in his business travels, and she welcomed the chance to spend some time doing things she enjoyed, like visiting friends, and checking on her younger brother.

As the stage doors opened, she nearly flung herself out and into the arms of her brother. "Billy!" Nora cried, hugging him tightly. "Let me look at you," she said, and pulled back slightly, then studied him critically.

Billy Madison, her younger brother, though not by much, had a grin on his face that could only be matched by hers. A gunslinger, Billy had mostly given that up in trade for a wife—the pastor's daughter no less—and ranching. Of course, trouble always had a way of finding Red Ridge, so he'd had a few adventures since that day, and hadn't fully hung up his gunbelt.

"How are you, sis?" he asked. "How's everyone back home?"

"They miss you, of course, but look forward to traveling here themselves soon," Nora answered. "Madeline especially sends her love. She's anxious to come and visit, but Mother made her go with her to assist Nannie and her little brood."

"I miss everyone," Billy said, "but I can't say as I'm in a rush to leave here. Something about this place just draws a fellow in."

"Would that something be Mirabelle?" Nora teased. "You can bring her too, you know."

"And scare her off with the lot of you?" Billy asked, pretending to recoil in horror. "She'd run so fast I'd never catch her."

"Oh, we aren't that bad," Nora laughed.

"Nope, you aren't. Especially you," Billy said, slinging an arm around her shoulders. "You bring many trunks? I've got three wagons. Should I get another?"

"Oh, you!" Nora said, smacking at him. "Just the two. Trunks, that is. That many wagons aren't needed. I'm sure you were teasing." She glanced around, just the same. Leave it to Billy to have actually brought three.

"I was," Billy said with a chuckle. "Just hitched up one. But they were on standby in case."

Nora rolled her eyes and pointed to the two trunks she had for her brother to lift onto the back of his wagon. "I was hoping Mirabelle would be here," she said, just a hint of disappointment filling her as she glanced around.

"She'd planned on it," Billy said. "But she was making some fancy dessert for tonight, and the oven was being too slow. She'll be watching out the window right now, I bet, looking for us."

"Then let's hurry," Nora said, starting to climb into the wagon.

"I thought you came to visit me," Billy said and crossed his arms.

"I did. In between visiting Mirabelle," Nora teased.

Billy laughed, and jumped into the wagon. He'd just shaken the reins when a horse came thundering past out of nowhere.

"Woah!" Billy shouted, pulling back on the reins and stopping the horses just in time as the rider came dangerously close.

"What in the world?" Nora gasped, clutching the edge of the seat tightly.

The horse stopped in front of the small building with a painted sign indicating it was the doctor's office. Someone must be in dire need of him. Nora's eyebrows drew together in concern.

"Wait here," Billy said grimly, handing her the reins and jumping off the wagon seat.

Nora could see Gavin coming out of the sheriff's office, settling his hat on his head. When he caught sight of her, he tipped the black Stetson and nodded, but joined Billy as they went to the rider who'd torn through the town dangerously.

"I've got to see the doc!" the man was shouting as he pushed past a woman to get to the door. His voice was so loud, Nora could hear his words perfectly, although he was across the street and already almost inside the building.

Billy and Gavin vanished inside behind him, and Nora waited impatiently, hoping nothing was wrong. A few moments later, her brother and the sheriff reemerged, and the rider mounted his horse, then flew off in the direction he'd come from.

Nora watched as a man with wavy dark hair just brushing his shoulders came out of the building, holding a doctor's bag. He mounted a second horse that was brought to him by a boy, one that must have come from the livery a few doors down, and followed the rider out of town at a fast pace.

"What was that about?" Nora asked as Billy came back to the wagon.

"No idea," Billy said. "Couldn't understand his stammering. Not sure the doctor could either, but he left too."

"That must be why the doctor had such a serious expression on his face," Nora said.

Her brother gave a slight frown, then shook his head. "No, that's his usual look," Billy told her, taking the reins back. "I don't know if I've ever seen him smile since he came to town a few months back. Aiden Rycroft, that's his name. He keeps to himself."

"I wonder why," Nora mused.

Her brother's voice turned serious, and Nora looked over to see his usually playful eyes much the same. "I've seen that look before on men," he said. "Usually when they've been struggling with something for so long, they're about to give up. Could be as a doctor, he's seen far more than he wanted to. Or it could be something else.

"Regardless, I don't want you going there unless you are hurt or injured. And even then, not alone. He's not been here long enough for us to know what kind of a man he is."

"You worry too much. Anyway, it's a credit to him that he still practices, if that's the case, that he's seen too much," Nora said.

Billy's head turned to her, and he narrowed his eyes. "Don't you be getting ideas."

"What are you talking about?" Nora asked.

"I'm talking about you thinking you should rush over and save him from whatever dark cloud is hanging over his head," Billy said. "I won't have it."

Nora laughed. "Where did you get an idea like that from? That's not something I'm prone to doing. You know that. I'm here to visit you, silly little brother. Besides, say I did take a fancy to someone. Are you going to chase them away?"

"I might," Billy said, his chin jutting out. "Not every man's good enough for my sister."

"I think I'll decide that for myself," Nora said, crossing her arms. "You didn't like it when Mirabelle's father acted the same toward you, so remember that."

"That was different," Billy argued.

"Was it?" Nora fixed him with the look their mother often used.

He stiffened, then said, "All I'm saying is you came here to visit. Not fall in love."

Nora sighed. "Billy, love is the furthest thing from my mind. So drop the subject before I push you off the wagon and you have to walk home."

Her brother scowled, but stopped talking. He knew she'd do it. But what Nora didn't understand was why he didn't want her near the doctor. Was the man fighting demons so severely that even her brother, someone who had seen and fought most everything, was worried?

Nora shivered, and turned her eyes to the scenery, taking it all in. Red clay soil, mountains off in the distance, and grasses mixed with small white and purple flowers. It was beautiful, and she was sure she'd never tire of being in Red Ridge.

"I'm glad you are here," Billy said. "I'm just...you know, wanting to look out for you." He shot her a sideways glance. "Can't have my favorite sister getting hurt."

Nora nudged him with her shoulder, but didn't answer. She was still filled with a little worry over the thoughts that had sprung up. Nora wasn't one prone to fits of imagination or emotion. She was as level-headed as they came, which was why she'd helped her father in his business when he'd asked her.

But she'd never known Billy to tell her something without good reason, so she wondered if his surface-level comment about wanting to look after her was the truth, or if there was more to it.

Billy cleared his throat. "Now, there's something else you ought to know. Being out here, danger's all around," he warned.

"I know that, but you'll always be nearby, so I feel quite safe," Nora assured him.

"There may be times I'm not," Billy told her, his voice serious. "So, there's something you need to be aware of. It's only a matter of time before it happens. You like your teeth?"

"What?" Nora held her hand to her mouth. "I don't understand the question."

The wagon hit a small hole and jolted. "I mean, you like having 'em?" Billy asked.

"Yes, I do," Nora said, feeling utterly confused.

"Then listen carefully. When Eli's kid, Meg, offers you something she's made, like a cookie, you've got to take it. He doesn't want any of us hurting her feelings. But here's what you do, so it looks like you are eating it, but you aren't..."

Chapter 2

"Come back in a week, and I'll check his stitches," Doctor Aiden Rycroft told the mother who had tears in her eyes and a small boy in her arms.

"Thank you, Doctor," she told him gratefully as she left.

As soon as the door closed behind her, the polite smile Aiden had put on fell from his face. He was tired. Moving here to Red Ridge had been a challenge he'd never expected. His biggest foe so far hadn't been outlaws or viruses or shortages; it had been boredom.

Other than small injuries, or the occasional cough or fever that wouldn't break, his patients were all robust, healthy, uncomplicated individuals. That was fine, and he was happy for them and their families, but it made for long days when his vast knowledge of the human anatomy and of medicines, herbs, and surgeries were not needed.

These stitches, on young Tom Winston who'd fallen on a garden tool while learning to walk, had been the most complicated thing he'd had in the last two months. Who knew when he'd have someone else come through his door? Sometimes, days passed between patients. How he would be able to stay here another few years under his contract, Aiden didn't know.

Yes, he could break it, leave. What would the town do? Nothing, likely. But pride wouldn't let him. He didn't need his family, in particular his younger brother, thinking he was flighty or incapable. His brother was their mother's favorite, the golden boy who won award after award, a celebrated doctor back home in Pennsylvania. He was also fond of sending frequent letters with his recent accolades.

Perhaps Aiden wouldn't feel so irritated if there were more to do. But all he felt was useless. He'd thought the West would be interesting and exciting when he came out here, but so far it had been quiet and peaceful.

While that wasn't a bad thing, it wasn't what he'd expected, either. What Aiden had wanted was a place to keep him busy. Keep his mind active. Allow him to make a difference in the community, and feel needed. A part of it. So far, none of that had happened, and he still felt like an outsider.

Aiden looked through the window at a person entering the sheriff's office. That was part of the reason there was very little excitement around here. It appeared that several local men, Eli Jones, Billy Madison, and the sheriff, Gavin Jefferson, were onetime gunslingers. Together, they had cleaned up the town more than once and considered it their duty to protect it, meaning that Red Ridge had a reputation of being a place that tolerated no crime toward its citizens.

That said, he supposed he should be grateful to the gunslingers. They did, on occasion, bring criminals to him to patch up before being transported to answer for their crimes. Those were generally easy jobs too. Bruises, a gunshot to an arm or leg. Nothing serious, as the men were excellent shots and knew just where to shoot to cause the least amount of damage while also disabling a person.

Aiden sighed, rubbed at his temples, and then rose from his desk. It was neat, orderly, just like everything else in his life. Would a little chaos, a little excitement, be so bad? Just for once? Why, he'd even settle for some hellos from the townsfolk as he walked to and from the office, but most just scurried on their way, silently.

He opened a desk drawer to get a dollar out and saw his brother's newest letter. It made him wince. Phillip had been accepted into a research program. Never mind he'd gotten in there using one of Aiden's old journals where he'd recorded, meticulously, the details of his own research on mold spores.

Aiden put the money into his pocket and left his office, locking the door behind him. Though the town was generally a safe place, he didn't want to risk someone going in and rifling through the medicines or other supplies there. It was difficult to get replacements, and it usually took more than a week for the most basic of orders to be fulfilled. Sometimes it took longer.

As Aiden walked down the sidewalk, his eyes landed on a woman in a pink dress, walking arm in arm with another woman. He knew the second was Billy Madison's wife, the pastor's daughter. Mirabelle, he thought her name might be. But he wasn't sure who the other woman was. Dark blonde hair, a pretty face, not too tall, and smiling. He was sure he'd have recognized her if she lived here. Who was she?

Just as soon as he asked himself that, Aiden realized that he had seen her. It was yesterday, as he'd rushed over to the Smith house where Mrs. Smith had fallen, and induced an early labor. This woman had been in a wagon, and Billy Madison next to her. Were they related? Or was she related to Mirabelle? He hadn't looked closely enough at either yesterday to tell, but he did let his eyes linger on the women now, as they walked into the general store.

There was something about the one in pink...he couldn't put his finger on it, but it was a feeling. Something that told him she was different. Special. Should be looked after. Which was why he needed to ignore her. A woman like that, she wouldn't ever be content with a simple man like himself. A doctor who got by, but wasn't wealthy by any means. Someone who served, wanting to make a difference rather than have fancy things.

Aiden shook off the thought, and pushed open the diner door. Madge, the owner, looked over at him from where she was wiping a table. "Welcome, Doctor! Sit anywhere."

"I'll have the chicken, please," Aiden said as he took his seat, pointing to the chalkboard Madge had with the daily menu. There was always a choice of two meals and two desserts.

"It'll be out in just a moment," Madge assured him, and then left to go into the kitchen. She wasn't alone in running the diner. Another woman named Lisa did the cooking, and yet another woman—who had actually replaced the sheriff's wife, Winnifred, when they married—had recently joined them. He couldn't remember her name. It might have been Joy.

"Here you are. I'll get your pie too. Peach or pumpkin?" Madge asked.

"Peach, please. But would you mind if I took the pie back to my office? I promise to return your plate," Aiden said. "I just hate to be away too long, in case I'm needed."

"Of course," Madge agreed. "I'll have it ready for you when you leave."

"Thank you," he told her, and tucked into his meal.

His mouth was full when the diner door opened a moment later, and Billy Madison walked over to his table.

"Doc," Billy said.

"Mr. Madison," Aiden replied after hastily swallowing. "Are you in need of my services?"

"No. Nothing like that. Mind if I sit?" the gunslinger asked. "And Billy is fine."

"Go ahead," Aiden said, a warning prickle running through his body and along his spine. "How can I help?"

Billy studied him from across the table. "It's none of my business," he began, "at least not directly. But, just now I saw you looking at my sister."

"Your sister? I wasn't aware you had one," Aiden said.

"She just went into the store with my wife," Billy said.

Ah. That was the other woman, then. Billy's sister. But why was the man here, talking to him?

"I see," was all he replied, and took another bite.

"She's..." Billy stopped, and rubbed at his jaw. "Well, ordinarily I wouldn't say anything, but I didn't care for how you were staring at her."

"With curiosity? Because I didn't recognize a stranger in the town?" Aiden asked, slightly sarcastically.

"No. It was more considering," Billy said. "My instincts are never wrong, which was why I came over here to tell you. Nora's not here to find a man. She's here to visit, and she'll be leaving before too long. I don't want her to leave with a heartbreak."

Aiden's jaw dropped. "I assure you, heartbreaking was not on my mind. Neither is any sort of acquaintance with your sister."

"Good. See it stays that way," Billy said, pushing his chair back. He left the diner without saying another word.

Aiden shook his head. He'd been truthful in all he said. He almost felt bad for the woman. With a brother like Billy Madison, she'd likely never marry. He didn't know what the man was worried about. He wasn't interested in her at all. His relationships in life were already complicated; he didn't need any more of them.

Chapter 3

It was a little chaotic at Billy's house, but Nora was quite sure she wouldn't have it any other way. She felt every bit a part of this large found family as she did the one she'd grown up in. It amazed her how the gunslingers were like brothers, and instantly welcomed everyone into their lives. Though she'd been there less than a week, they and their wives treated her as though she'd always been a part of Red Ridge.

Eli, Hannah, and their children were there tonight, as were Gavin, his wife Winnie, and her siblings. Old Gus had joined them, and was tapping one foot to Gavin's violin playing, while Eli strummed at a guitar. Hannah's new baby girl, only a few weeks old, was being passed around and cooed over.

"Care to dance?" Gus asked Nora.

"I'd be delighted," Nora said, and soon found herself being whirled around to the lively music.

"It's right good seeing you again," Gus told her, spinning them around. He linked arms with her and led her toward the left. "Hope you can stay a spell. You looking to settle here?"

Nora spun the other direction, slightly breathless. "I don't know. I'd like to. Something about this place feels like home, but I can't impose on Billy and Mirabelle for too long."

"Doubt they think you impose. But if you're worried, why don't you find a fellow?" Gus asked. "You're purty enough."

The music came to a stop, and Nora took a moment to catch her breath. "No one has caught my eye," she told him, but then she teased, "what about you? When will we see you settle down? Make some woman a good husband?"

The old ranch hand blushed so brightly, it was all Nora could do not to laugh.

"Well, now, I might have my eye on a woman," he said, "but not sure she knows it yet."

"You'd best tell her," Nora told him. "That's the only way she'll know!"

Gus nodded, but he looked a little uncertain. "Saw another man hanging around. Got myself a little nervous feeling now."

"Why don't you take her some flowers?" Nora suggested.

He brightened. "I ain't done that yet! That's a right good idea. My weather knee is telling me tomorrow will be sunny. Think I'll do it then."

Nora squeezed his hands. "I hope it works." She smiled at Gus. "Thank you for the dance. Goodness, I'm tired! I'm going to sit this next one out."

"That's just fine, because Gus is mine now," Winnie said as she took her turn spinning about while the music played.

Nora clapped along, but soon found herself seeking the shadows that were beginning to fall. Gavin's violin stopped as Gus and Winnie's younger brother Nick broke out harmonicas and played another tune.

Nora watched everyone laughing and having a good time. Little Meg was dancing with Eli. He was so good to her, Nora mused. Not every man would treat another's child like his own, but he was completely her pa, and she had him wrapped around her small fingers.

"What are you thinking about?"

Nora startled, surprised to see Gavin next to her. "Just watching everyone," she told him.

"I can tell something's on your mind," he said.

It was likely true. Gavin was the quiet one. The deep thinker. That let him see others in a way most wouldn't.

He was also good to be with, if one simply wanted a companionable silence.

Nora sighed softly. "I was just feeling...out of place. There have been a lot of changes for me in the last few weeks, and I have found myself trying to figure out where I fit in now. What I should do."

"This town is a good place for that," Gavin told her. "It'll come. And we'll all be here to help you."

"Help you what?" Billy asked, coming up on her other side.

Gavin nodded at her, and then walked away, giving them privacy.

"Help me figure out my place," Nora said. "With Father not needing me, my choices are to find a job, or join Mama and help Nannie." She hesitated, then said, "Well, I suppose there's the other option of me settling down, but I'm not sure I'm ready for that yet."

"You don't need to work," Billy told her. "I've got plenty."

"I do too," Nora said. "But it's not about money, little brother. It's about feeling useful and finding my place in life. Surely you understand that."

He nodded. "I do. But I also know that things happen in the timing they should."

Nora raised a brow. "Aren't you the philosopher," she said.

"Pastor Blackstone said that on Sunday," her brother admitted. "We sit right in the front row, Mirabelle and me, with her ma."

"Ohh, so you can't fall asleep," Nora teased.

"I don't fall asleep in church!" Billy said indignantly.

"Of course not," Nora laughed. "I bet Mirabelle pinches you if you do."

"Knitting needles," he muttered. "Keeps 'em in her handbag."

After their laughter faded, they stood in silence for a few moments, watching the dancers.

"Go join the others," Nora said.

"Can't leave you here alone. I can tell you've got worries on your mind," Billy said.

"I'm fine, Billy. I just want to enjoy the fresh air and the night sky that's starting to fill up. It's been a long week. There was all that travel too, and I'm plumb worn out," Nora told him. "You know me. I'm also not used to being around so many people. A few moments alone are just fine by me."

He nodded uneasily, and then walked a few steps away. Billy paused, and then asked, "You'd tell me, though? If you needed me for anything?"

It was on the tip of her tongue to remind him she was older than he was and had been taking care of herself for a long time, but Nora saw the concern and the brotherly love on his face, and simply nodded. Somewhere along the way, her little brother had grown into a caring man, and she was grateful for it.

Nora was also grateful that someone did care for her. Her mother was so focused on their other sister and her two sets of twins, and her father his business and his new decision to sell it, often it felt as though she were simply trying to keep things running smoothly for others, even at the cost of all she had within her. Nora was no stranger to long, exhausting days, or working until her eyes were bleary. But she couldn't recall anyone ever noticing or worrying about that. Except for her brother. He always had.

She realized Billy was still waiting, and gave a small nod. "I promise. And you know, I'm really glad to have you as my brother. There's no one better."

He grinned then and gave her a wink. "There sure isn't!"

Billy walked over to Mirabelle, and Nora stepped back deeper into the shadows. It wasn't that she wanted to be unsociable, but she wanted to be alone with her thoughts. Seeing everyone happy, their futures laid out, their hearts—even Gus's—matched to another...it made her feel a little lost. Lonely.

Tomorrow, she'd walk into town and inquire as to who might be hiring. She needed something to take her mind off of that feeling. Billy was right in that she didn't need to work, but she did need to feel useful.

And...if she was being honest with herself, there was something else she wanted to do. Wander past the doctor's office, and see if she could get another glimpse of the man. For some reason, she couldn't stop thinking about Dr. Aiden Rycroft.

If it was because Billy didn't want her near him or because something about the man drew her in, Nora wasn't sure. But she hoped that short glimpse she'd had of him when she arrived a few days ago wouldn't be the only one she got.

Chapter 4

Aiden looked through his window. He had a good view of the street. Two boys were playing with a ball, throwing it back and forth near one of the stores. He frowned. That was asking for trouble. They really shouldn't be doing that in the town, not when there were other areas better suited.

Aiden was about to return to his book when his eyes fell on a woman walking along the sidewalk. He couldn't see her face clearly, but she hadn't noticed the boys, instead looking into the distance at something else.

One of the boys threw the ball, just as the other bent over to tie his shoe. The ball flew right toward the woman's head. In an instant, Aiden was out his door, just in time to hear the shattering of glass and the cry of pain from the woman.

He hurried over to her and was surprised to see it was Billy Madison's sister. The sheriff was only a few feet behind him.

"Nora!" the sheriff said. "You're bleeding."

The woman looked in surprise at her hands. There were small cuts on them, but her face had taken the worst of it. "Why, so I am," she whispered. "What...what happened, Gavin?"

"Boys playing ball in the street," Aiden answered. "When the ball broke the window, the glass shattered and struck you. Miss Madison, I think you'd best let me check your wounds and be sure there's no glass in your skin. You can't see it, but you've quite a few cuts on your face, and one looks particularly deep."

"I agree," Gavin said.

"Yes, please," the woman said. "Thank you."

"I'll let Billy know," the sheriff called as they walked away.

Miss Madison paused at his words. "There's no need. I can take care of myself."

"He'll want to know," the sheriff said. "And he is on his way to my office, anyway."

Aiden didn't miss the small sigh and the resigned nod of Miss Madison. They walked to his office, and he led her to the examination room. There, he busied himself with getting clean cloths, bandages, and medicines to both clean and treat her wounds.

"I am hoping nothing is so deep it requires stitches," Aiden said. "My apologies for needing to get so close, Miss Madison." He moved near her, leaned in, and carefully studied her face. She had eleven small cuts, and two larger ones.

"Nora, please," she told him.

Aiden liked the sound of her voice. It was sweet, warm, rich. A contrast to most of the other women he'd talked to.

"I'm just checking for any shards," he told her, gently running his fingertips over her cuts. He'd visually inspected, but wanted to be sure nothing else remained.

Beneath his fingers, Nora sucked in her breath. He was going to ask if he'd hurt her, but his throat was too tight and the words wouldn't come loose, no matter how he'd willed them. Her skin was so soft, and there was a hint of jasmine coming from her hair. Aiden found his fingers trembling and pulled away.

Taking a deep breath, he said, "No glass embedded in your face. Let me see your hands, and then I will clean these cuts."

She offered her hands, and he examined each carefully, then used a pair of tweezers to remove a small piece of glass from the back of one hand. As before, he gently ran his fingers over her cuts, feeling for anything his eyes might have missed.

If he lingered a moment longer than he should have, Aiden didn't know. He just knew he didn't want to release her hands.

"Thank you for helping me," Nora told him. "I'm so grateful to you, Dr. Rycroft."

"Aiden is fine," he told her. "Please."

What he didn't say was he wanted to be on a first name basis with her. Her brother's warning came into his mind, but he pushed it away. After today, it was unlikely he'd have contact with Nora again. She'd probably leave for wherever her home was soon, and he...he would be left with this moment. But no complications. Just as it should be.

Reluctantly, he released her hands, and then cleaned the cuts and carefully dabbed ointment on them. "No stitches," he told her. "You are lucky. I don't foresee any scars either. I'll give you a bit of this ointment to take with you. Apply it twice a day to improve healing."

"Even if I were to scar," Nora said, "it wouldn't matter. I'm not vain. I do, however, wish I'd had a better story for all of these cuts. Not paying attention to my surroundings doesn't sound very exciting. It's a shame that's what happened."

As she laughed, Aiden couldn't help but chuckle himself. Nora Madison seemed nothing like her brother. She was delightful. Perhaps that's why the gunslinger had been so worried. In truth, if he had a sister such as her, he might also be overly protective.

"I'll be done shortly," Aiden promised, and gently dabbed at her face.

She sucked in her breath sharply as he worked on the largest cut. One near her eye. "I'm grateful you weren't struck any closer," he said, examining it critically. "Another inch, and your eye could have been damaged."

"It's a wonder I wasn't," she murmured, and then walked over to the small mirror to study her face. She turned her head slightly from side to side. "I'm a sight, aren't I?"

Aiden didn't know how to answer that. He wanted to tell her she was beautiful, but knew that wouldn't be appropriate. He also didn't know why he was suddenly so enamored by her. He'd treated plenty of female patients, and never once found himself thinking such a thing.

So, he answered, "It could have been far worse, but I imagine it will give your brother a shock."

"Yes, I think it will," Nora said, still studying her face. Through the mirror, she met his eyes. "I imagine you thought I might get all emotional, being a woman."

"If you had been, you'd have no judgment from me," Aiden told her. "Tears and emotions are tools we humans have to cope with fears and stresses. Male or female, we all have those emotions. Some doctors cry as well, did you know that?"

"I did not," she said, looking surprised.

"It's true. Not in front of our patients, but sometimes we do. I was taught tears are a way of honoring the struggle someone else goes through. They are also a way of mourning a loss. Or grieving that you did all you could and it wasn't enough."

Her eyes were locked onto his. "I hope you have not had many of those instances," she said quietly. "I can tell, just in the few moments I've talked with you, that you are the kind of man who does all he can to help his patients."

Aiden wasn't sure how to answer her, but he was spared, as his office door flew open suddenly, and Billy Madison rushed into the examination room.

"Nora!" he said, all but shouting as he grabbed his sister's shoulders. "Are you okay?"

"I'm fine," Nora said. She nodded toward Aiden. "Thanks to the doctor here. He was there just seconds after it happened, and has patched me up."

"Yes, and let me get you some of that ointment to take with you," Aiden said. He turned to the jar and began to scoop some into a small tin.

"Nora, go on out," Billy said. "I'll be right there."

"Something you want to say you don't want me to hear?" Nora asked, raising her brows. "Oh! That hurts. Hold on, let me try a scowl." One passed over her face, making her look even lovelier, if that was possible. "That's better. It doesn't hurt to do that."

Aiden tried not to smile at their sibling interaction. He would never have guessed she had this kind of sass in her.

Her brother just sighed. "Please?"

"Fine." Nora walked past her brother, but then stopped at the door. "Thank you again, Aiden, for helping me. I'm most grateful for your care."

"You are welcome," Aiden told her. "Here is the ointment."

Their fingers brushed as she accepted the jar. Did her fingers linger? He wasn't sure. Her brother's thundercloud of a facial expression was starting to make him nervous.

Then she left, as did the faint wisp of jasmine floating on the air behind her. Aiden held back his sigh as he turned to the gunslinger. "She needs to apply it twice a day," he said. "If you need more, I'm happy to supply it."

Billy nodded. "Thank you. But just so you know, this doesn't change things. I don't want you around my sister. You're new here. No offense, but I don't know what kind of person you are. Not yet. And Nora...she's important to me. I nearly failed once," he said, "I'm not letting anyone else special to me get hurt."

"I understand," Aiden said with the polite smile he gave his most irate patients, even though he had no idea what the man was talking about. "As I said before, you've no reason to worry. If it makes you feel better, I'll even charge you. It will be fifty cents."

"Good," Billy said with a nod, as he dropped the money into Aiden's palm. "Business only. How it should be."

As the gunslinger left, Aiden scowled and dropped the coins into his desk drawer. He couldn't stand the man. Not one bit. He hoped he'd see Nora again, but knew he'd be keeping his distance. He had to. He didn't want a gunslinger or his friends coming after him.

Once more, Aiden regretted coming to Red Ridge. Now, he'd be stuck here for years with more than just boredom. He'd be trapped with memories of a woman he couldn't get close to, no matter how much he might want to. Heaven help him the next time he did see her. It would be all he could do not to talk to her.

Chapter 5

"I wish you hadn't done that," Nora said, as she rode behind her brother on his horse. When he insisted she get on, or else he'd walk, she climbed up, and hoped the beast wouldn't be too burdened. "You embarrassed me. Likely the doctor, too."

"I didn't mean to," Billy said. "But you didn't see how he was looking at you when I came in! I don't know if he's a good enough of a fellow to be looking at my sister that way!"

Nora's jaw dropped. She was pretty sure her cheeks were flushed too, but was glad her brother couldn't see. Had the doctor really been staring at her in such a way? She wasn't opposed to the idea at all.

Billy, however, was.

"He was looking at me," she told him, "with concern. That's it. We were discussing the fact that another inch, and I'd have had glass in my eye."

She could feel her brother tensing. "Gavin's given those boys quite a talking to, I'm sure. He will be taking them home and talking to their folks as well."

"I feel badly for the shop owner," Nora said. "It will be days before his glass window can be replaced. But don't you be changing the subject, Billy. Do you forget, I'm older than you? While I might be visiting you, I make my own decisions. Don't make me do something rash or out of spite because of how you are behaving."

"You wouldn't!" Billy said, trying to twist around to see her.

"Try me," Nora said, knowing full well her eyes were flashing. "You completely embarrassed me, sending me outside like you owned me!"

"I'm sorry," Billy said, lowering his head slightly. "Just, after what happened to Mirabelle, I get a little nervous when people I don't know too well start looking at the women in my life."

She couldn't blame her brother for that, and some of the heat left her voice. "What exactly did you say once I left?" Nora asked.

"I told him thanks."

"What else?" Nora gave him her best older sister look, even though she was sure he couldn't see it.

She could feel her brother squirm. He might not have been able to see her look, but he could feel it. "Nothing."

"Liar."

"Look, it's my job to take care of you," Billy said. "You're my sister, and my guest. And...well, gosh darn it, Nora. You know what happened to her. You think I'm going to risk anything like that happening to you? My sister?"

Nora pressed her lips together. She wasn't going to argue any further. Billy had a valid reason for why he'd done what he had. She just wished he hadn't ever gone through such a thing.

She rested her head against Billy's back and closed her eyes for a moment. Her head was starting to hurt, and all of the gashes were stinging. She wanted to rest, and perhaps put a cool cloth on her injuries.

"Just not sure he's good enough for you," Billy muttered.

"I am not looking for anyone," Nora reminded him, trying to ignore the flutter she'd felt when the doctor's hands had been on her face, on her hands. She'd hardly breathed, her chest was so tight. His soft touches had left far too soon, though she knew he'd let them linger.

Was it possible...had he felt something too? If she was looking, she knew Dr. Aiden Rycroft was just the man she'd consider.

"You know," Nora said, as Billy's home came into view and took her from her thoughts, "you aren't the only

Madison with good instincts. We each have inherited them from Mother and Father. So, I think it's time you trusted me to trust mine."

Billy dismounted, and then helped her down. "What are yours saying?" he asked.

"That there's a good deal to that doctor others don't know about, but deep down, he's a good person," Nora said.

Her brother's lips pressed together. That familiar gesture that she herself often did. It made her wonder now if all of her siblings did it.

"I'll trust you," Billy said. "But that doesn't change my opinion right now. I want to keep you safe."

Nora stood on her tiptoes and kissed Billy's cheek. "I know you do, and I love you for it. Keep an open mind," she told him. "That's all I'm asking." She studied her brother's face for a moment. "Just so you know, the next time I see the doctor, I plan to thank him again." She winced. "And potentially ask for more ointment. My face hurts. I'm going to see if Mirabelle will lend me a cloth I can dampen to dab at these cuts."

The rest of the day, thankfully, was just the three of them, and there was no objection when Nora said she wished to retire early. She applied the ointment to her cuts, wishing it was the hands of the doctor, who smelled of nothing but good, clean soap, that touched her face.

It was difficult to sleep that night, and in the morning, Nora blamed the discomfort of her face and hands—not the fact she kept thinking about the doctor's eyes and his gentle voice—for her yawns.

"What are your plans today?" Mirabelle asked over breakfast.

"I've got to ride with Eli to look at a head of cattle," Billy said. He stood and kissed his wife on the cheek. "Hope you ladies don't mind, but I'd best go now. He's likely waiting on me."

Once Billy had left, Mirabelle turned to Nora. "I was going to visit Winnie for a while with my mother. Her sister had some questions about becoming a teacher. While I don't have much experience with that, my mother was one before she married Papa. Would you like to join us, or would you rather stay here?"

"Would you mind terribly if I didn't go?" Nora asked. "I thought...well, I thought I might visit the doctor again."

"Oh no!" Mirabelle gasped. "Do you feel worse?"

"I feel about the same," Nora said. "But I want to thank him. And also apologize. Billy rushed in yesterday, and..." She shook her head.

"Ah, no need to explain," Mirabelle said. "After what happened, when he gets protective, he doesn't always think when he talks. Still, he's a good man, and you've a fine brother."

"Yes, he is," Nora said. "I wouldn't change him for anything, and I'm so happy he is the way that he is. After all, he saved your life. But," and her voice lowered as she admitted, "the doctor and I were having a conversation, and I...I..."

Nora stopped. She didn't know what to say. How to finish her sentence. But Mirabelle just gave an understanding smile, and rested her hand overtop of Nora's. "No need to say another word. Go on, but promise to let me know if anything interesting happens!"

With a laugh, Nora agreed, and then got herself ready to go into town. She didn't put on her nicest dress, but she did choose a soft green one that she knew made her hazel eyes a little brighter.

Once again, the weather was nice, so she chose to walk instead of taking one of the horses. Only, this time, she'd be paying close attention to her surroundings, especially by glass windows.

When she arrived at the doctor's office, she hesitated, and then opened the door. Aiden looked up right away from where he'd been leaned over a book, and rose from behind his desk.

"Nora," he said. "I wasn't expecting to see you so soon. How are you feeling?"

"The cuts sting," she admitted, "but the ointment you gave me soothes them."

"I'm glad to hear that," he said, leaning against the front of his desk. "What brings you in?"

"I wanted to thank you again," she answered, trying to ignore the rapid beating of her heart. If it kept pounding, she'd be tempted to ask him to check her pulse.

"I was just doing my job," he told her. "Nothing more."

"May I take you to lunch? As a thank you?" Nora asked.

He raised his brows. "I've never had a woman offer that before."

"Then you've obviously never had a woman grateful enough that you helped her," she teased. "Perhaps you should try harder."

He laughed, and it made his eyes light up. She liked that. Liked the sound, and the expression now on his face. He still hadn't answered, though, so she stepped closer.

Nora didn't know why she did it, but she rested her hand on his arm gently. "Will you?" she asked. "Please?"

"Your brother..." he started, and then hesitated.

"Has no business interfering with my decisions," Nora said. "I have told him that. He is protective. Perhaps overly so, after what happened with Mirabelle."

Aiden shook his head. "I am not aware of that story," he said.

"Then join me at the diner, and I'll tell you all about it," Nora said.

"Are you always so pushy?" Aiden asked.

He didn't say it in a way that was accusing, but more in surprise. Amusement. She noticed the tiny quirk of his lips.

"Sometimes. It runs in the family, I'm sure you've noticed. Does that mean yes?" Nora asked.

"Let me get my keys to lock up," Aiden said and, as he walked past her, Nora could have sworn his fingers brushed against hers. Her legs felt like jelly, and as she met his warm eyes as he stood by the door, Nora felt lighter than she ever had in her life.

She was also incredibly glad for those two boys playing ball. They'd acted as the perfect intermediary for her and the doctor.

Chapter 6

Aiden tried not to feel nervous as he sat across from Nora. Her invitation to lunch had been very unexpected. And, now that he was with her, the conversation was every bit as good as the company and the meal.

Nora's voice was pleasing, and he enjoyed the small talk they'd had while waiting for their lunch of vegetable stew. He was surprised to discover that Nora had spent time in a medical office, assisting her uncle who was a doctor. That explained part of why she hadn't been squeamish when he'd treated her.

As Nora reached for one of the flakey biscuits and broke it in half, slathering it with butter, Aiden took the opportunity to venture, "Are you staying in Red Ridge long?"

Quickly, he added, "I ask because I wanted to make sure if you leave soon, you'll have someone able to look after your wounds." He struggled to keep his voice even. Polite. Professional. Uninterested. Had it worked?

"I'm not sure when I will leave," Nora said, a thoughtful expression on her face. "I'm at a crossroads right now in my life. It's my hope to figure things out while I'm here."

"How so?" Aiden asked. "If I'm not being too inquisitive, I mean."

"Not at all," Nora assured him. "You see, for the last twelve years, I helped my father with his business, doing his books, running errands for him that included a little travel. All of the busy work that he wasn't able to do. But now, he's selling the business, and I am finding myself at a loss as to what I want to do next."

"Are your parents open to letting you choose for yourself?" Aiden asked.

"They are," Nora said. "I am...older, and as I've not married yet, it feels a little awkward to entertain the idea of finding my way now, especially as most my age are already settled."

"There's nothing wrong with marrying late or not at all," Aiden said. "I am nearly thirty-two, myself, and unmarried."

"I am twenty-nine," Nora said, gracing him with one of her smiles.

"That means you've been helping your father since seventeen?" Aiden asked, doing the math quickly.

"Longer, for his books," she admitted. "Father mixes up his numbers when he writes them or reads them, so I have been his second set of eyes since I was perhaps ten."

"Interesting. A few weeks ago, I was reading about a German physician who was studying what he might end up calling word blindness. It sounded similar, only with letters getting mixed up, not numbers. I am sure your father appreciated your help," Aiden said. "A noble thing to do."

"Nothing noble about helping one's family," Nora said, and took a sip of her tea. "I am just grateful that our father has always accepted his female children were just as intellectual as his male. But what of you? When I came to Red Ridge previously, I don't think you were here. I remember a much older doctor, though I can't recall his name."

"Yes, I took his position, and as it seems he was just the last in a long line of doctors. I also signed a contract, promising that I'd be here for a minimum of three years."

"How unusual," Nora said, her eyes widening. "But, at the same time, I can understand. Red Ridge had some difficulty with the underhanded folks who had been here before. Perhaps they are hoping that with a good doctor, and a few other steadfast and honest businessmen and citizens in the town, people will settle here again, and grow the area."

"You might be right," Aiden said. And, when Nora said it, it made him feel a bit better about his position here. He was doing more than just treating patients. He was encouraging the town's growth. That didn't solve his problem of being bored by lack of patients, but one thing at a time.

"Did you leave many friends or much family behind?" Nora asked.

"My parents and a younger brother," Aiden said. "They are still in Pennsylvania. It was good to get away, though. For me, this was a much-needed change, even if it's drastically different from what I imagined."

"I bet it is," Nora said. "Might I ask what you wanted to get away from? Or is that private?"

Aiden would tell her anything she asked, he realized. In fact, he'd do most anything—even risk her brother's anger—to keep talking with her. How had he started to feel this way so quickly?

"My family is full of expectations," Aiden said. "While I met them, somehow I was never quite good enough. That crown went to my younger brother, Phillip. The charismatic one. I'm as dour as an old woman, my mother would say. Phillip was the favorite. But he..." Aiden stopped. He wasn't sure if he should say more.

Nora spoke then, picking up her spoon. "I am not an only child," she reminded him. "I know all about sibling rivalry. Is that what you are alluding to?"

"Yes," Aiden sighed. "I suppose so. My brother would often use my research and present it as his own. At first, I was hurt and angry. But eventually, I just let him. It was easier that way, even if the bragging wasn't."

"That's terrible," Nora said. She reached across the table and took his hand. "No one should feel they have to put up with such deception, just to bring peace to their family."

Aiden gently rested his other hand on top of hers. When she didn't move, just looked at him with her mesmerizing eyes, he admitted, "But I can say good has come of it."

"How so?" Nora nearly whispered.

Aiden hesitated. Dare he say what he was thinking? Who was this man, sitting here in his place? What of the promises he'd made about not getting too close to her? Not complicating things?

"I met you," he finally answered.

The flush that spread across her cheeks made him do the same, and Aiden would have laughed at the situation, was he not feeling so infatuated with Nora.

Another couple came in, and he and Nora reluctantly returned to their meal.

"I understand you are in a difficult situation," Nora said. She frowned, and swirled her spoon around in her bowl. "I worry that my parents won't be happy unless I quickly decide what I want to do. They aren't ones for idle behavior. Hence my decision to find a job, though Billy isn't keen on the idea."

"I'm not too keen on your brother," Aiden said dryly. Then he quickly stammered, "I'm sorry. That was terribly rude of me."

To his surprise, Nora just laughed. "It's quite all right," she assured him. "Billy is a good person. Usually the first to make a joke or laugh, and he's very lighthearted. But after what happened to Mirabelle..." Her voice lowered. "That's right, you are unaware of the story, as it happened before you arrived."

Aiden's brows knit together. "I'd welcome the chance to hear it," he said.

"This was more than a year ago," Nora said, "before they married. It actually started just before I came to visit the last time. Mirabelle and Billy didn't know each other yet, beyond glances. But there was someone else Pastor Blackstone wanted her to marry, who he thought was another pastor's son.

"However, the man turned out to be a criminal, leading a gang. They intended to hold up the bank, as I recall. This man held the Blackstone family prisoner, cutting them off from any help. Mirabelle and I didn't know each other then, but when I saw her, something made me pretend we did.

"She begged me to pass word along for help. I did, to Billy. And then, the man kidnapped Mirabelle. Billy was frantic. When he found her, the cabin the gang kept her in caught fire. She was still inside."

"My word," Aiden gasped. His jaw hung open, but he didn't care. This explained a lot.

"Billy rushed in, along with Gavin and Eli, flames all around them, and saved her." Nora was quiet. Her face was so pale, Aiden could see a few faint freckles on her cheeks. Nora took a deep, shuddering breath. "The outcome could have been far worse than it was. The entire situation was devastating for the Blackstones, and for Billy.

"I think it may have set many of the townsfolk on edge. After all, if a man appearing to be a pastor's son could trick them all and was in fact a criminal with a gang, and kidnapped a woman...what next?"

Aiden sat back in his chair, slowly shaking his head. "I had no idea. It's understandable, especially if as you say the town was in the grips of other unlawful behavior, that others would be suspicious and wary around those they didn't know. Not just your brother."

"Yes," Nora said. "If you just give people a little more time, they will continue to warm to you."

"Perhaps that's why I have not had many patients," Aiden mused. "Here, I thought it was just the town was unusually careful and lucky." He glanced at Nora with a sheepish expression. "I was feeling rather wasted as a doctor, truth be told. But now things make more sense."

She nodded. "I can see where you could. I'm glad you now know why. I think in time, the others will start to see what I see in you."

Aiden wanted to ask her just what she saw in him, but before he could say anything, Nora whispered, "A man who cares deeply about what others think, and a man who I am starting to care for."

She sat back suddenly, her hands flying to her mouth. "Forgive me. I am mortified. I don't know what came over me. You must think the worst of me right now."

"Not at all," Aiden said, rushing to assure her. "I also now understand why your brother said you are special. I think so too. And I..." His voice dropped. "I would like to get to know you better, if I may."

Chapter 7

Nora hummed to herself as she walked down the sidewalk. Lunch had been lovely. She'd enjoyed talking with Aiden, and was disappointed when it was time to say goodbye.

As she neared the sheriff's office, she saw Gavin talking to Gus, and slowed down. "Hello," she greeted them.

"Afternoon," Gus said, tipping his hat.

"How are you?" Gavin asked.

"Good," Nora said, sure her blush gave her away. She was still feeling as though she were floating on clouds after her lunch with the doctor. Just then, her eyes landed on Gus's newspaper, and tension filled her. "May I see that?" she asked.

"Of course," the old man said and handed it to her.

"I've got to help with the stage," Gavin said. "Prisoner on board." He tipped his hat to her and left.

"Fever and Ague Spreading," Nora read from the headline. "Is this Red Ridge's newspaper?"

"It ain't," Gus told her. "A few towns over. But Glinda over at the general store gets them for me."

"I see," Nora said with a frown. "That sounds worrying, though."

"I'm sure there's nothing to be concerned about. 'Sides, we got a doc, if needed."

"Yes, we do," Nora said. "Well, thank you, Gus. I've got to be going. Have a good afternoon, and give Hannah and the children my love."

She left, slowly walking away, and wondering if she should perhaps mention to the doctor about the outbreak. Fever and ague was not something small. It could wipe out entire towns. The fever came first, followed by terrible chills, headaches, and muscle weakness.

Nora wrapped her arms around herself tightly. Perhaps Billy would know more, if this was indeed going to be a threat to the town. If so, perhaps they could stock up on any medicines they might need to protect themselves.

She soon arrived at his house. Mirabelle wasn't back yet, so Nora took the opportunity to write to her mother and send her love. When a short time later she heard someone enter the house, she left her room, and headed down the stairs.

"Hey, Sis!" Billy said. "I thought you'd be with Mirabelle."

"I sent my love and apologies," Nora said. "Truthfully, I just wasn't up to it."

"I understand. Sometimes those get-togethers are tiring. A man wants a little peace and quiet." Billy laughed. "Listen to me! Sounding like Gavin!"

"Speaking of him," Nora said, "on my way home, I saw him and Gus. Gus's newspaper was from a few towns away, and the entire front page was about fever and ague sweeping through the town."

Billy's eyes flickered with concern. "Is that so?" he asked. "I wonder how close it is."

"I'm sure he'd let you read it," Nora said. "My concern is, what can we do in case it comes here?"

"Well, it might not," Billy told her. "So we shouldn't be worried." But his eyes still kept their seriousness.

"You are thinking something," Nora said. "Tell me."

He looked around, as if to make sure they were alone, and dropped his voice. "The man we got the cattle from told us the person who owned the cattle died. Matter of fact, his whole family was wiped out from fever." Billy shuffled his feet. "Don't think animals get it, but soon as we heard that, Eli and I quarantined the entire herd. We'd have done it anyway, but have a whole pasture between them. Gonna keep them that way for a month. Just in case."

"The whole family," Nora whispered, pressing her hands to her heart. "Oh, Billy! This could be bad."

"Don't I know it," he said. "I'm fixing to ride and ask Gavin his thoughts. Eli and I already talked it over. We want to keep a close eye on things, maybe get the doc to stock up a little on whatever medicine is needed in case it heads this way. Now, after hearing what you said, I'm convinced it's the right thing to do. But we don't want to upset or scare anyone, so we're keeping quiet for now."

"I understand. That's a good idea," Nora said. "So is seeing that the doctor is stocked up."

"Just stopped to change my horse," Billy told her, and turned to leave. Then he paused, and, as though it were almost painful for him, asked, "Would you like to ride along with me while I visit the doctor?"

Impulsively, Nora hugged him tightly. "Yes, please. I'm very concerned about this. I'd had the same thought, preparing just in case." She stepped back. "Give me just a moment to get ready."

"I'll hitch the wagon," Billy said, and disappeared outside.

After quickly washing her face and checking to be sure none of the cuts were seeping, Nora joined him. They rode to town in silence, until Nora said, "I had lunch with Aiden today."

Her brother stilled. Then he asked, "Did he behave?"

"Yes. Billy, I enjoy being around him."

Her brother let out a deep sigh. "Are you sure?"

"I am."

He was quiet, then finally said, "I'll try to be nicer."

"Thank you," Nora said, and smiled at him. "That's all I ask."

Billy grumbled, "But at the first sign of him misbehaving...me and Eli and Gavin are going after him. I promise you that."

"I wouldn't expect anything less," Nora said. She let out a little sigh. "I don't think I'll ever have a man riding to my rescue. But it sounds nice. Romantic even."

"It's a darn sight scary on the man's end," Billy said, "though I'd never admit that to anyone else."

"You're a good man," Nora said. "I couldn't ask for a better brother."

"You couldn't get one even if you tried," Billy said with a shrug. "That's a fact."

Nora laughed, happy that all seemed to be going well. She was enjoying her time in Red Ridge, looking forward to the possibility of something with Aiden, and now, she and Billy had gotten past his mistrust of Aiden. At least, she hoped. She knew it would be a hard thing for Billy to fully set aside his concern for her. After all, he was used to being the one looking out for others, but she did hope he'd try with Aiden.

If something did come of their growing friendship—

"You see that?" Billy asked.

Nora glanced around. "No, I missed it."

"Town's not very busy," he said with a frown. "School's let out. But the kids aren't playing."

Fear started to trickle in through Nora's veins. "Something feels wrong," she said quietly.

"Real wrong," Billy agreed, as his eyes flicked around the town. "Let's see the doc, and then I want to check in with Gavin."

He parked the wagon, set the brake, and then helped Nora down. They went into the doctor's office.

Nora could hear Aiden with a patient.

He called out to them without looking, "I'll be there shortly; just have a seat."

She and Billy sat in two of the chairs and waited, listening.

"Take her home, and have her rest. Willow Bark tea, cool rags on her head. If the fever persists, let me know, but most fevers tend to break within a few days on their own." Aiden walked the patient out, a woman who had her arm around a young girl, perhaps eight or nine.

"Thank you, Doctor," the woman said, leaving.

Aiden turned toward Nora and Billy, and then looked surprised as he recognized them. "Good afternoon," he said.

"Afternoon," Billy answered. He nodded toward the door. "Is that the first fever you've had this week?"

Aiden walked toward his desk. "Do you mind if I sit? Since I came back from lunch, there's been a stream of people. It's most unusual."

"Go ahead," Billy said, leaning forward a little. "All fevers?"

"That's the strange part," Aiden said. "Yes. For the most part. There was one severed finger I reattached. But yes, almost all children, and all with fevers. What surprises me is most people choose to treat those at home and not see a doctor. But they are coming in droves."

Nora exchanged a look with her brother. "Billy," she whispered.

Her brother pressed his lips together. "Doc, Nora read in the newspaper from a few towns over that fever and ague are sweeping through. The man Eli, Gavin, and I bought cattle from today was a broker. The man who had owned them, and his entire family, were wiped out by fever shortly after we'd paid for them."

The doctor closed his eyes for a moment, then reopened them, saying, "I'm glad I'm sitting. Do you suspect it's in Red Ridge and this is the source of the fevers?"

"I don't know," Billy said slowly. "I'm not a doc. But as we rode in here, there was a strange feeling. It's making the hairs on my neck stand up, and that's never good."

Aiden reached for a sheet of paper. "Well, if it's as you suspect, once you've left I'll make my notes about these patients even more detailed and watch closely."

"If it is the fever and ague," Nora asked, "how would you treat it?"

"Time," Aiden told her. "And quinine." He rose and went into the other room. "I'm checking my supply of it now."

Billy followed, and Nora watched from the small waiting room. "You got a lot on hand?" her brother asked from the room's doorway.

"Average, I suppose, for the usual needs. But perhaps I should send away for more. This isn't enough to treat even a fraction of the town."

"Might not be a bad idea," Billy said. "I'm heading over to see Gavin. You can expect him to stop by later," he warned. "There are a lot of families on the edges of town who might not be able to get here if something's wrong. We may need to send people around to check on them. See if this really is something to be worried about, or just a coincidence."

He started to the door. "You ready?" he asked Nora. Then he stopped. "Actually," he took a deep breath, "You say your goodbyes. Meet you at the wagon in just a moment." He looked as though he were wanting to say something else, but then left.

Nora felt gratitude fill her, and she turned to Aiden. He was walking toward her, surprise on his face.

"I didn't expect him to do that," he said.

"Which part? Ask about the illnesses and medicines? Or leave just now?"

"Leave, and let me have a moment with you," Aiden said. "I know he and his friends are very protective of the town, yet I admit, I am a little surprised he'd be so concerned about an illness coming through."

"They care deeply for everyone here," Nora said. "It's rare, but wonderful."

Aiden nodded. He searched her face then. "Don't worry about the fevers. I'll write to the other towns within fifty miles and see what their doctors have to say. I'll also order medicines from my suppliers. You, however, you stay safe. Don't get near anyone who looks ill, has a fever, or is shivering. Wash your hands frequently, and dry them well afterward."

He closed the distance between them, and whispered, "If I've just found you, Nora, I don't want to risk losing you."

She closed her eyes as his hand came to her cheek, and leaned into it. More than anything, Nora wished he'd embrace her. Even kiss her, but the moment she thought that, she couldn't believe herself. They hardly knew each other. Why would she think such a thing?

He dropped his hand, and turned toward the door as another parent came in with their child. Nora knew now, there was no doubt about it. Her heart was longing for him, and as their eyes met just before he walked into his examination room, Nora knew that she was just as worried about the fevers finding him as he was about them finding her. She might be able to stay isolated, but Aiden...he was the doctor. And right in the middle of some sort of epidemic.

Chapter 8

When the door closed behind the patient, Aiden sank into his desk chair. Almost immediately, he rose and went to the bookshelf, where he kept his medical books. Selecting several, he returned to his desk, flipping through the pages.

Fever and ague. That was another name for malaria. And, if it was true that it was spreading, there was a good deal to be concerned about. No one knew how it spread, though superstitious folk believed it was from the night air. All he had in his books and journals were the symptoms—fever, followed by chills or shivering, intense sweating, joint pain, body pain, headache...the list continued.

What was frustrating, was many of the symptoms his patients today had, could be attributed to many things, not just this fever and ague. A common virus, for example. Dust in the sinuses. Heat exhaustion.

Aiden tapped his fingers on his books thoughtfully. Still, better safe than sorry. The West had fewer supplies available, and it took longer to get them. He'd best put in an order.

He carefully looked through each book to see what it suggested for treatment. Again, the information was similar. Quinine appeared to be the best. However, it might be difficult to procure such a large quantity as one might need to provide for an entire town, including those on the fringes of Red Ridge.

There was another concern, as well. Even if he could get as much as he needed, the issue with quinine was it was ground from the bark of the cinchona, and so was not a liquid. The bitter taste—not that medicine should taste good—made it difficult to mask, and even harder for some to take, as they knew the taste would be off-putting.

And for a person who was incredibly ill and perhaps unconscious, spooning the life-saving medicine into them was often a difficult task. There was not a standard dosing, either, like some other medicines, such as morphine, had. That made one uncertain if they were giving enough or too little.

He would simply have to get as much as he could by sending an urgent request to the two places where he got his medicines from.

Just as Aiden lifted his pencil to the paper, his office door opened, and a man walked in.

"Can I help you?" Aiden asked, standing.

"Need some advice, Doctor. My wife and baby, they've been poorly. Fever, about three or four days. It's not going away." The man gripped his hat in his hand. "I don't know what to do. Don't have no one else to turn to."

Aiden felt his chest tighten, but he kept his tone even, like he'd been taught in medical school. He replied, as though they were discussing the weather, calmly. "Have you done cool cloths on their heads?"

"Yes, sir."

"Tea to keep them hydrated? Willow bark can help with fever."

"Yes, sir."

"Are they shivering? Or sweating?" Aiden asked, walking into his examination room.

"Yes, sir. Some of both."

Reaching for his bottle of quinine, Aiden swallowed hard. The bottle was only half full, but he'd arrived with it as such and hadn't even touched it until now. It wasn't something he frequently needed. He poured a little of the powdered bark into a small vial, then turned to the man.

"Return to me in three days, and tell me if this has worked," he told him. "Or, if it has not. You will mix a very little bit of this into something for your wife to drink.

Perhaps a drop for the babe, no more. It is usually not given to infants."

"Thank you, Doctor," the man said, taking the vial. "What do I owe?"

"Fifty cents," Aiden said.

The man fumbled in his pocket, and dropped the coins on Aiden's desk, hurrying out.

Aiden returned to his desk, and the letters he'd started just before the man had come in. Quickly, he scribbled out his request for as much quinine as could be gotten, and urgently, and then folded and sealed the letters.

On his way to the post office, Aiden looked around him at the streets. Did they seem quieter than usual? He wasn't sure and didn't want to jump to conclusions based on his speculations. It was a hard thing to do, and something that he'd often struggled with as a physician. It was important to be understanding, calm, and factual with patients, who were often emotional.

But it was an entirely different thing to be that way himself, when he knew if there was to be a large outbreak of an illness, he was but one man with limited supplies. The very thought of it was, truthfully, nearly overwhelming.

Aiden stopped at the post office and waited his turn. When he got to the window, he slid the letters over the counter. "These are most urgent," he said. "Can they be sent right away?"

"Can go out tomorrow," the postmaster promised. "The rider will be here at dawn."

"Thank you," Aiden said, and left. He debated stopping in at each of the general stores to see what herbs or medicinal remedies they might carry, but if he did, that might tip off or alarm the proprietors. No, best to stay quiet about this. Instead, what he might do is scour his books to see what other herbs might be beneficial for fever, and check his supplies of those.

As Aiden returned to his office, he watched another couple walking arm in arm. It made him wonder if he and Nora might one day do that. He hadn't expected to feel the way he did toward her, especially with her overprotective brother, but he felt so different when he was around her. Happy. As though the constant weight settled on his shoulders had vanished.

Though he'd only known her a short time, Aiden knew without a doubt she was the best thing that had ever come into his life. Her brother had even seemed to soften a little. Maybe he was just acting that way around Nora, trying to be nicer, but maybe not. Now, if they could just get through this potential situation.

Aiden's thoughts came to a sudden stop as he saw two people waiting outside of his door. "I'm coming," he called. "Apologies, I had to post a letter. How can I help you?"

While he treated the patients, and two others who came in after them, there was little time to think about anything but the fact that fever and ague might well have come to town—and they had very little medicine to treat it. Suddenly, Aiden found himself wishing for those moments the days before, when he was bored and feeling unneeded.

Something told him it would be a long time before that happened again.

Chapter 9

Nora peered into the small mirror in her room with relief. Not only had the cuts on her face healed in just over a week, they wouldn't leave any marks. She wasn't vain, she'd been truthful in telling Aiden that, but it would be nice not to have to explain to people over and over what had happened.

Nora smoothed her hands over her dress and then left her room. Today, she was joining Mirabelle for tea with her mother and Callie, Mirabelle's best friend. She was looking forward to what she hoped would be a quiet and relaxing afternoon.

"The wagon's ready if you are," Mirabelle said as soon as Nora got down the stairs.

"Yes, I am. I'm sorry if I've kept you waiting." Nora quickly headed toward the door.

"Oh no, not at all," Mirabelle assured her as she followed. "I'm just excited to go. Since Callie got married, she's hardly had time to see me. I'm glad she's able to join us today."

"Yes, it will be nice to see her and your mother," Nora said, settling herself into the wagon.

Mirabelle flicked the reins, and a short time later they were at the Blackstones' house, a cozy little building right next to the church.

The doors of the church were open, and Pastor Blackstone's voice trickled out. It sounded like he was practicing his sermon for Sunday.

"Welcome, welcome," Mrs. Blackstone called, opening the door of her house. "Callie just arrived."

Mirabelle hugged her mother, while Nora squeezed her hand. The pastor's wife hustled them into the sitting room, where a lovely assortment of small sandwiches, slices of cake, cookies, and tea awaited.

"It's so good to see you!" Mirabelle said, hugging Callie tightly. "How is married life?"

"Quite fine," Callie said with a smile. "It's more difficult to take care of a house than I imagined."

"Cookie?" Mrs. Blackstone asked, bringing around a plate. Nora accepted one, and then her eyes fell on Callie's wrist, as her sleeve moved up slightly.

"Have you hurt yourself?" Nora asked. "That bruise looks quite bad."

Callie stammered, "No, no, I just... it's nothing, really." She tugged on her sleeve to cover the mark.

Mirabelle's sharp gaze fell on her friend. "You'd tell us if it was more, wouldn't you?"

Callie's gaze fell to her lap, where she smoothed an invisible wrinkle. "You needn't worry about me. Look at us both," she said with a bright smile as she looked at Mirabelle. "The two of us married, with homes of our own, and enjoying tea! Why, when we were children we dreamed of this while playing tea party!"

"Yes, you did," Mrs. Blackstone said, and started to tell a story about one of those times.

Nora didn't bring up the bruise again, but she wondered if she should mention it to Mirabelle later. There was no way the woman could have done that to herself or had it happen by accident. Judging by the way Mirabelle kept glancing at her friend, she also felt that way.

When there was a lull in the conversation, Nora asked, "Mrs. Blackstone, I'd heard that the fever and ague was in nearby towns. Have you heard of many people here with fevers?"

The pastor's wife nodded. "I have. There seems to be something spreading, though I'm not sure what, and Pastor Blackstone and I have been praying around the clock. I went today and bought extra flour, so that I could make loaves of bread and deliver them to those houses."

"I will help by doing the same," Mirabelle said, concern in her voice. "I wonder why Billy didn't mention anything."

"He might not have known, dear," Mrs. Blackstone said. "After all, people are more likely to ask the pastor for aid of a spiritual or physical nature than a gunslinger." She let out a little giggle. "A gunslinger! I never imagined my daughter being married to one! It still makes me laugh each time."

Mirabelle joined in the soft laughter now in the room, and then added, "That might be it. Or else he didn't want us to worry." Her eyes filled with concern. "You will let us know if we can help beyond that, Mama?"

"Yes, I will. I think that's a wonderful idea to help bake more loaves. Your father was going to give as many as I can bake to the homes affected by the sickness."

"I'll make extra dough tonight," Mirabelle promised. "You can count on me to make a dozen each day until you tell me to stop."

"I will help you, Mirabelle. Perhaps we can increase the number. I hope it's nothing serious going around the town," Nora said, pressing her hands to her stomach as worry filled her.

"As do I," Mrs. Blackstone said, "but remember, girls, this is all in God's hands. Even if we don't see a reason for it, He does. That does not excuse us, however, from doing our part to aid those who need us."

The women murmured their agreement, and the conversation turned again, this time to who was expecting, but though Nora nodded and chimed in on occasion, her mind stayed on the potential threat facing Red Ridge, and the question of what the town might do if such a thing did spread.

She longed to visit Aiden, to see if he'd been able to get more quinine, but it wouldn't have been polite nor seemly to leave, and since she'd come with Mirabelle, she couldn't very well drag her sister-in-law along with her to speak to him or leave without her.

Nora knew Billy had known there was the potential for this, so why hadn't he said anything to Mirabelle? Had he forgotten? Or was he trying to save her from worry? In truth, she suspected the former. Billy was never dishonest, but if he was distracted with something, an illness sweeping through another town might not have been foremost on his mind.

It also could have been he was so preoccupied with making preparations, he neglected to mention it to his wife, thinking he already had. Either way, word was spreading, and Nora had the feeling they'd need as many loaves—and as much medicine—as possible.

Restlessness washed over her. She stifled a sigh, and nodded as the conversation turned again. Nora smiled when the others did, and laughed along with them, even if she didn't know everyone they talked about and her mind was quite distracted. She tried to stay focused, but it was rather difficult, and she found herself longing to leave, to speak to Billy or Aiden or Gavin, to find out what news there was in the town.

Though Mrs. Blackstone plied them with the sandwiches she'd made, Nora found her stomach had soured, and she felt like she was choking with each bite her dry mouth tried to take.

Her mind kept thinking through the fact that no one knew what caused fever and ague, so no one knew how it spread, only that not everyone recovered.

If this sickness did come to Red Ridge, how many people that she'd seen would be gone? What if it was someone she was close to? Billy or one of his friends, or their wives? Aiden, who would be on the front line of care.

The idea made a lump form in her throat, and Nora busied herself with refilling the teapot in the kitchen in order to hide the tears that were forming.

"Please, God," she whispered as she looked through the window to the small town beyond. "Spare us all."

Chapter 10

The jar of quinine had been empty for two days. Those early individuals who'd been fortunate enough to get some had recovered significantly. Which meant that this *was* malaria.

And Aiden had nothing more to help them with. People would die. There was no way around it. Some would recover, even without the medication, but others wouldn't.

He tried not to think about what he'd learned in medical school. How, in 1830, it was reported seventy-five percent of the Indians, right here in Oregon, in the vicinity of Fort Vancouver, had died from the disease. By the time the illness stopped spreading, ninety percent of the Chinook and Kalapuyan tribes had passed away. Almost thirteen thousand lives. Malaria had decimated them.

Though modern medicine had come a long way these last thirty or so years, even one life lost in this town would be too many. And without medicines, there would no doubt be deaths, for those whose bodies were too weak to fight on their own.

"God help us all, if our numbers are as great," Aiden whispered.

Between his patients that morning, Aiden wrote two more letters, pleas once again for help and medicine to his suppliers, and stood, preparing to take them to the post office. It was also time to tell the sheriff of the need for more medicine, and see if perhaps he could help some in this situation. He'd heard the former gunslinger had contacts in many places. Hopefully, he could help with this.

How was it there had been no answers? Were his letters not getting through? Or was there simply none of the medicine to be found? Aiden didn't know which, but either was a concern.

He started to the post office, but at the last moment veered, heading to the sheriff's office instead. The soonest the mail would leave was tomorrow. But perhaps the sheriff had a way to get the letters there quicker. It didn't hurt to ask. The worst that could happen was he mailed them himself.

As Aiden went into the sheriff's office, Sheriff Jefferson looked up at him. Eli Jones, another of his friends and a gunslinger, nodded hello.

"Doctor," the sheriff said. "What can I do for you?"

"Help, I hope," Aiden said grimly. "Sheriff Jefferson—"

"Gavin," the man interrupted. "I understand you and Nora are friends. A friend of hers is on a first-name basis with me."

"And I'm Eli," the other gunslinger said. "The same goes for me. Now...if you make her cry..."

Aiden swallowed. Billy was already a worry. Were these two as well? "Thank you," Aiden said, trying to ignore the implied threat. Upsetting Nora in any way was the furthest thing from his mind.

He held up the letters. "I have been writing for help. This is the second time, to the usual suppliers of my medicines. I'm sure you've noticed, we have a good number of folks sick right now."

"Do you think it's fever and ague?" Eli asked. "We've been concerned ourselves."

"I do, because the little bit of quinine I had helped the ones I gave it to." Aiden's lips pressed together, then he said, "But I have had no answer to my letters, and we must get more. People may die without help." His voice lowered. "They might still die even with it, but we stand a better chance if we can get the medicine."

"And you are out of it?" Gavin asked.

"Yes." Aiden looked between the two men. "I have given every granule of what I had. Those who had it recovered, likely because they got it so swiftly. I need help. Help to get more medicine. Help to be sure my letters are getting to their destination. It seems strange I've had no reply."

"I'll take them," Eli said, reaching out his hand. "You can be sure they will get there. Gavin, will you tell Hannah I've gone? I don't want her worrying." He glanced at the letters. "Look for me tomorrow with whatever news I may have."

The sheriff nodded. "I will. I'll also ask Pastor Blackstone and Billy to start counting how many families are ill, and see if we can get a few more able bodies to join in. Door to door but keeping a distance, since we don't know how contagious this is. I know the pastor had been visiting and taking bread, but we need actual numbers.

"Aiden, I'll stay in town in case things get out of hand. You're doing the best you can, and you have little to work with. Some folks might not understand that, though, and get riled up. I'm not going to let them threaten you. And, if Eli gets the medicine, I won't let them swarm you. I'll keep things orderly. Fair."

Aiden nodded, feeling a little bit of surprise, as the men quickly formed their plan and included his protection in it. This wasn't what he'd expected, but he was grateful. He also hadn't thought about the last part, how others might be angry with him, even though his hands were also tied.

Or how they might overwhelm him once he did have the medicine, not letting him properly divide it.

A hurting human could be the nicest person ordinarily, but under stress, being fearful, they could be dangerous.

And the knowledge of how many people needed care could aid him in rationing the quinine appropriately, once he got it, though he greatly disliked the thought he might have to choose who got it and who didn't.

But with someone delivering the letters in person, well, Gavin was right. Eli might even be able to bring it back with him. If not all, at least some.

For the first time in a few days, Aiden felt a little flicker of hope.

"Thank you both," he said.

"Don't thank us yet, Doc," Eli said.

"Aiden, please," he answered. He rubbed at his eyes. "I appreciate the help."

"This town is under our care," Gavin said. "These are our people, and we'll look after each of them as best we can."

"I will be back at my office," Aiden said, a yawn escaping him as the first shot of hope that day infused him and made him relax. "In case I'm needed."

He started to leave, when the sheriff said, "Aiden. Hold up. You been getting rest?"

The question surprised him, and he stopped for a moment to think about the answer. Was he? When had he last slept more than a doze?

"Actually, not very much," he admitted, once he'd thought about it. "I've had so many patients, I've been sleeping a few hours here and there at my office, since they are coming at night now for help."

"You need another pair of hands," Eli said. "This is too much for one man."

"There is no one else," Aiden said. "And we don't know how this sickness spreads. It's my job. I won't put anyone else at risk."

The two men exchanged looks, and Eli said gently, "As fine of a doctor as you are, you won't do anyone any good if you collapse. Nora would be a fine nurse."

"No!" Aiden nearly shouted. At their surprised looks and raised brows, he stammered, "I-I can't let her. If she gets sick..."

The sheriff studied him a moment before he answered. "You like her more than we thought. That'll make Billy relax a little."

Aiden didn't answer. Had they been discussing him and Nora as well? He wasn't sure what to think. Luckily, Eli said, "There's time for that later. I'm going now. Good thing I rode my fastest horse today." The gunslinger went to the door. "Good luck. I have the feeling we're going to need it."

Aiden hurried outside after him, and tensed once he saw a patient waiting at his door, slumped on the bench outside.

Yes. Luck. That was something they were in desperate need of. He prayed the gunslinger would find it and bring it back with him.

Chapter 11

Nora stopped to drink a cool glass of water and shake out her hands. Her fingers ached from what seemed like the neverending kneading of bread dough she and the other women had been doing all day. Hannah and her children had just gone home, as had Winnie and her sister. It was getting close to dinner, and everyone was tired and hungry.

It was good to know she was helping, and losing herself in the mindless process allowed her to think. Since she couldn't be with Aiden right now, she could do the next best thing. Think about him.

"Just a few more," Mirabelle said wearily. "Then we can load them up for Papa to take. I'm glad I put that pot of beans on to simmer this morning."

"Me too. Nothing like baked beans drizzled with molasses," Nora agreed. "It's nice not having to have to worry about cooking, since you had some leftover cornbread from yesterday."

Was Aiden eating? She hoped so. It sounded like the man wasn't able to set foot outside of his office now. Was he able to sleep any? Her mind suddenly filled with worries for him, and she longed to see him, if for no other reason than to assure herself he was well.

Gus stuck his head in just then. "Got you womenfolk two more sacks of flour," he said. "Want them in here?"

"Might as well," Mirabelle said. "We'll be making more bread tomorrow."

Though the women had considered making soup as well, they had neither enough jars nor an easy way to transport them. The bread, however, was much simpler to deliver. They were making sure to make large, hearty loaves, as many as they could.

"Do you think Eli will be able to bring back medicine?" Nora asked Gus. "Any news from town?"

Hannah had been worried, though she'd not said anything, when Gavin had stopped by a few hours before to tell her Eli had ridden off to be sure the request for quinine reached the suppliers for Aiden.

"If anyone can, it's one of these men," Gus assured her. "Don't you be fretting none."

Nora nodded, but fretting had been just what she'd been doing. There was a knock at the door, and Mirabelle went to answer it. She returned a moment later with Gavin. Nora was surprised to see him there, instead of at home.

"I wanted to tell you something," Gavin said, a serious look on his face.

Stilling, Nora wiped her hands on her apron. She didn't miss that Mirabelle and Gus left the kitchen. "Is Billy okay?" she asked. Though, if something had been wrong, she was sure he'd have told Mirabelle first.

"He's fine. Still going around getting a count of how many need help," Gavin said. "I was able to catch him and the pastor a while ago, and he'll be back in an hour." He gave her a considering look. "What I didn't tell you earlier was I spoke with Aiden."

Her heart fluttered. "Oh?"

"He needs help," Gavin told her bluntly. "If he doesn't get it, he's not going to be of any help to anyone. He's got more people lined up than he can care for. They're coming at all hours, and he's been sleeping between patients, there in his office, since they come at night too."

"That's terrible," Nora said, biting her lower lip. It was as she'd feared. "I had no idea there were so many."

"As sheriff, I feel compelled to find him help. I talked with Billy," Gavin continued. "He agreed with me when I said you might be the only one the doc considers letting help him. But, before you answer, Nora, it puts you at risk."

"I will go at once," Nora said, starting to the door.

"Wait. No, in the morning. You need to think about this first."

"I don't need to," Nora said firmly. "In this town, we are all family." She hesitated. "But Billy...he won't be upset, me spending entire days with him?"

"He's worried about you getting sick," Gavin said, "but it was part his idea. He told me how you helped back home, when sickness came through."

"It's true I have helped before," Nora said. "It wasn't anything like this, but we all did. Since the doctor was my uncle, it only seemed natural to assist when my aunt, his nurse, became ill."

"That makes you the most qualified of all of us," Gavin told her. "The others can keep making bread for us to deliver. With any luck, we'll be delivering quinine with it soon."

"I just hope Aiden will let me help him," Nora said, sighing. "I get the feeling he's a little stubborn."

"Oh, I figure you've had plenty of experience with that." Gavin chuckled. "You're a Madison, after all. Got a streak of it yourself I bet."

She laughed. "I think you are right."

Gavin headed toward the kitchen door. "See you later," he told her.

Once he'd left, Mirabelle came back in. "What will you do?" she asked.

"You were listening?" Nora asked, putting her hands on her hips.

"Of course. We're friends. Saves you the time of telling me," Mirabelle said, her eyes wide.

"I will offer help, and hope he allows me," Nora said.

"Hannah sure wishes she could do more," Mirabelle said. "But with the baby, we all understand. She also can't risk getting close to anyone sick."

"No, she can't," Nora agreed. "But will you be fine, making the bread without me?"

"Of course," Mirabelle said. "Don't you worry."

Nora nodded, and lost herself in her thoughts of how best she could convince Aiden to let her help as she and Mirabelle worked silently.

After a quiet dinner, she wandered to the porch. Off in the distance, she could see Gavin and Winnie's house, and faintly heard Gavin playing his violin.

The long, low notes were mournful. Just how she felt. There was movement next to her, and she looked over as Billy sat wearily.

"How bad is it?" Nora asked.

"Could be worse, but it sure isn't getting better," Billy said. "I'm worn out. Used up all my smiles and jokes for the little ones to set them at ease when I visited."

"You'll recharge overnight," Nora said, hoping if she teased him a little he'd smile. "Can't keep a good man down for long."

"That's for sure," he agreed. Then he fixed her with a look. "You going to help the doc?"

"Are you sure you don't mind?" Nora asked. "I know you had concerns."

He sighed deeply. "I do. But he needs help. More than that, I think he needs you. That's what Eli says, anyway. He wrote me a note before he left. I reckon if he and Gavin think the doc's all right, so can I. What kind of man would I be if I said no? Can't be selfish when the town—and he—needs you. But you take care of yourself."

"I have to," Nora told him. "I love you too much to send Mother after you if I get sick."

They laughed softly together over that, before Nora heard her brother say, "I mean it, Sis. Couldn't stand it if you..." He couldn't finish.

"I don't plan to," Nora told him. "But if I do, and it's because I helped a dozen people recover, or two dozen, it's worth it. I'll have no regrets, Billy, and I wouldn't want you to feel any guilt. You hear me?"

"I know," he agreed. "I'd say the same. Why do we have to be so selfless, us Madisons?"

She didn't have time to answer with a joke, because he stood, slapping the porch railing. "I'm off to bed. It's early, but I'll be up early. Going to hit the other side of the town tomorrow. Riding with Mirabelle's father again."

She nodded, and once her brother had gone inside, Nora sat, until so many stars had filled the night sky she couldn't count them anymore. When her eyes tired, she went to her bed, and wondered if Aiden was getting any sleep. She hoped so. But more than that, she hoped he'd accept her help.

Chapter 12

His eyes were so tired they burned, but Aiden didn't once slow down. Madge over at the diner had been bringing him meals and coffee and tea. He'd tried to pay her, and she'd shooed him off.

"We all do our part here in Red Ridge," she'd said firmly. "You're helping the town, and I'm helping you. Once things get back to normal, you can pay for meals you eat there. Until then, none of that kind of talk. Besides, a lot less folk coming in for meals right now. Don't want it going to waste, do I?"

He was grateful for the meals. Too tired to take time to leave and seek a meal or cook one, he knew he'd credit Madge and Lisa's meals with keeping him going. He wouldn't have been able to maintain his energy with only bread and cheese.

He'd had just enough time to bolt down his meal before the next patient came in. However, false hope and advice for the fevers was all he could offer them.

"Any day now, and we'll get you the medicine, I promise," he told person after person, writing down their names on a sheet of paper that grew longer by the day.

His door jingled, but before Aiden could stand and force the smile on his face, Billy's voice called out. "Sit. Just me. Came to see how you were."

Aiden hadn't expected him, and dryly said, "I'm sure a week ago, I wouldn't have expected you to ask."

The gunslinger laughed. "Tell you the truth, I wouldn't have." He perched on the edge of Aiden's desk. "Got to tell you something."

"I'm listening," Aiden said, curiously.

"I took a liberty," Billy said slowly. "I hope you won't be mad. Gavin thinks it needs to be done. He's sheriff, so that outranks best friend when it comes to the town's welfare. Fact is, you need some help around here."

"I'm managing," Aiden said. "Though I appreciate the offer, you and I both know that to have someone here could put them at risk. I'm already praying I don't catch whatever this is. Hence, the windows open at all times to circulate the air."

"And I get that," Billy said. "Which is what makes what I have to say even more difficult."

Now Aiden was really curious. He studied the man before him, observing his posture. For the first time he'd ever seen, Billy looked as though he'd lost his confidence.

Billy looked into the distance, through the window that overlooked the town, but it was obvious his eyes weren't focused on any one thing. "When we first came here and helped Hannah," he said, "we promised to protect the town once we'd realized what had happened. It was also a good excuse to settle down together.

"When Gavin took the oath of office, he swore the same. To always do what was right by the people here. Regardless of any of that, the three of us, we've been friends a long time. So, what one does, the other is likely to do."

He was quiet, and Aiden waited, wondering what he was trying to say.

"It's a mighty hard thing to sacrifice, sometimes. Even when you know it's the right thing to do." His eyes snapped to Aiden. "We've got a nurse for you. She's done this before. Not this exact thing, fever and ague, but sickness sweeping through a town. She'll be a fine help for you."

Aiden started to rise from his chair. "I told you—"

"It's Nora."

He fell back into his seat, speechless. And then he quickly said, "I can't allow such a thing. She can't. If something were to happen, then I—"

"You need the help, Aiden. You know you do. You can't visit the worst folks at their homes while keeping the office open for those close to town who can make it here. Facts are, you're just one person, and she'd be a help. Not just to you, but for the town."

His head lowered. Was this the first time Billy had called him by his name? He took in a deep breath, then met the gunslinger's eyes. "You are right. I do. But not Nora. I can't protect her from this if she's here. And I know you want her to be safe as much as I do."

Billy studied him a long time. Finally, he said, "And that's why I know you're the right person for her."

"What?" Aiden's breath came fast, and hard. "I'm not—"

"Neither of you are," Billy said, standing. "But one day, you might be." He walked to the door. "Just keep her as safe as you can. She's my sister, and I love her. Nora...she's the best part of our family. But it would be selfish of me to keep her from you and from the town, when I know how much she can help you and help them."

Aiden didn't know what to say. He couldn't speak right now. His mind was spinning with confusion.

Billy opened the door. "We each got to fight battles how we do best. Mine's with a gun. Yours is medicine. Nora's is her ability to help others. She'll be here tomorrow morning."

And as the bell signaled his leaving, Aiden watched through the window as the gunslinger strode through town, nodding and waving to those he passed. Aiden shook his head. He hoped he wasn't coming down ill. Surely, the man hadn't said what he thought he had.

But just as certain, Aiden knew that even if Nora did come, he'd refuse her. He had to, to keep her safe.

"I don't need her," he said. Then he crossed his arms. "I don't need anyone."

It wasn't true. He knew it. Even his words sounded uncertain to his ears, but Aiden didn't care. That was his truth. He'd say it over and over until he believed it.

All that mattered was protecting the town of Red Ridge, and that included Nora. It especially included Nora.

The sun was going to set soon. He had no idea where Eli was, and if the man had even found the destinations to pass off the letters. He hoped he had and was on his way back with the promise of medicines.

Time passed. Surprisingly, no patients came in. He would take this reprieve. Whether it was because there were no new cases, or this was a calm before the storm, Aiden didn't know. But he'd take the moment of relaxation.

Stars started to dot the skies, and Nora came to mind. He wondered what she was doing right now. Was she maybe looking up at the stars as well? Sending up a wish for something? Someone?

Aiden let out a deep sigh, and pushed himself up from his desk, moving to the examination room where he spread his blanket on the table and lay down. The moon shone through a crack in the curtain, and he stared at it, willing his exhausted body to sleep.

It couldn't, though. Not when the door opened, and he heard the frantic cry of, "Doc? Please help us!"

Chapter 13

Nora came down the stairs, pausing as she heard voices coming from the porch through the open window. She was dressed and ready to head to town. Mirabelle was going to take her as she dropped off the bread they'd made the day before to her father. More loaves were rising now, waiting to be baked when she returned.

She nodded hello as the front door opened, and Gavin walked in with Winnie. Billy followed behind.

"Well, hello," Mirabelle said, coming from the kitchen.

"I wondered if you wanted to have some company while you baked," Winnie said. "My sister is studying, so I thought I'd come over and help. Truthfully, this is hard for Lily. It reminds her of our parents' illness. And, I know Hannah won't want to leave until Eli comes home, but she'll be baking bread there with Meg. I just didn't want to be alone."

"Your help will be appreciated," Mirabelle answered. She reached for her friend's hand. "Are you doing all right, Winnie? I know this must bring up some memories for you as well."

Nora wasn't sure what Mirabelle meant. Winnie must have sensed that, because she turned slightly, so she was facing both of them and including Nora in her nod.

"I'm fine. You are right, it does bring up painful memories, but I have so many good ones now, I know I am blessed." She gave Nora her attention. "Years ago, a sickness spread through our town. A quarter of the population was lost. My parents were among them. To make a long story short, my sister, brother, and I were sent to an orphanage. It wasn't easy there, or for the time afterward, but we are reunited now, and all is well. Still, this..." Winnie bowed her head.

"I'm so sorry," Nora said. "And here you are, helping others to go through the same."

"I am glad that I can," Winnie said, truth in her voice.

"I was just about to take Nora into town, and drop off the bread to Father," Mirabelle said.

"I can do it," Billy offered. "Then he and I can take our wagon around today, and we won't have to take that rickety one he borrows."

"Thank you," Mirabelle said.

"I'm ready whenever you are," Nora told her brother.

Gavin kissed his wife goodbye while Billy did the same to Mirabelle. Nora tried not to feel that tiny tug of sadness that there was no one special who'd miss her while she was gone.

As they walked outside, Gavin shook his head. "This is frustrating. It's a time when our guns or our fists can't fix things."

"No," Billy agreed. "But our dollars can help. Be sure if anyone mentions they need something, you send them our way. Maybe we ought to make a town charity fund."

"That's an idea," Gavin agreed as he mounted his horse.

There was no small talk as they rode to town. They were silent, each lost in thoughts. Nora was glad for that. She wasn't sure what kind of welcome she'd have from Aiden, nor did she know what to expect when she walked inside. That made her a little nervous.

As they pulled up, she quickly climbed down the wagon. "I'll walk home," she told her brother.

"Nah, I can get you," Billy answered. "I figure I'll be with the pastor all day, and end about the same time as you. Besides, you need to conserve your energy."

She nodded, and faced the doctor's office. Tinges of nervousness filled her, but she started toward the door. Behind her, she could hear the wagon rolling away.

Nora pushed open the door and walked inside. Aiden was sitting at his desk writing. He looked up as she walked inside.

"Nora," he said, giving her a tired smile.

"You look exhausted," Nora said. "Where can I start? How can I help?"

He shook his head. "I'm managing fine. Really. I told your brother I didn't need help."

"Those circles under your eyes say differently," Nora said. "It's obvious you are getting no rest."

"I get enough to sustain me, and when this is over, I'll have more."

"I'm not so sure about that," Nora said doubtfully.

He looked around, as if to see if others were nearby. "Truthfully?" he said, "when I close my eyes, I see patients. Frightened parents of sick children. Husbands or wives, terrified the next breath will be their loved one's last." He swallowed hard, and she saw his Adam's apple bob. "It is almost a relief not to sleep. I think these nightmares will stay with me."

"They might," Nora said softly, coming around and resting a hand on his arm. "It's a hard thing to be a doctor, I suspect."

"The older I get," he said quietly, "and the more I see, the more helpless I feel. We are all fighting battles internally or externally. My job as a doctor is to help ease them as much as I can. But how, when so many are not a foe I can defeat with a medicine or an ear? Too many battle demons, struggle just to get by, suffer from losses. And now this... I cannot help, even with medicines because I have none.

"I became a doctor because I thought—foolishly—I could make a difference. But there are some things we can't fix. I can't fix. Things I have no control over, even if I am a doctor. And that's a terrible feeling, being helpless when you want to make a difference."

"But you already do," Nora told him. "I wish you could see that. Those who leave here have hope, which is more than they came in with."

"I'm not sure I make enough of a difference. Maybe that's why I want to spare you from this idea you have of being here, helping me. To save you from heartache. The frustration of doing your best and it not being good enough."

Aiden stood, and began to pace. "Nora, people will die. Some who walk through these doors and who you assist. That will be a hard thing for you. You'll wonder if you did enough. Could have done more."

Nora shook her head, willing the tears that burned behind her eyelids not to come to her eyes. "I'll gladly accept it, for the moments when I can do good. In any form I would suffer, because it will have meant that my efforts, even if they failed, existed. That I lived, and I tried with all I could. That I comforted, and I mourned, and I celebrated, and I loved.

"Don't you see, that is why I am here? Why I think you are here? I will do all of these things. With or without you and your help. If you don't want me here, I'll travel door to door with Pastor Blackstone. But..." she drew in a deep breath, and reached a hand toward him. "I'd like to be here with you."

Tiny muscles in his jaw clenched, and Aiden's voice dropped lower. "This is a lonely profession."

"Then we can be lonely together." Nora pointed to the examination room. "Go. Rest for a time. I'll be here to help."

He took a few steps, and Nora thought he was going to listen to her, to go rest, but instead, he drew close and put his hands on her elbows, then slid them up to her forearms.

"Nora," he whispered, "I couldn't stand it if something happened to you. Please. Leave. Go somewhere safe."

"I won't leave you to this alone," Nora told him softly. "Not when I can help you. Don't you see I worry for you as well?"

He sighed, and rested his forehead against hers. "Is there nothing I can say to convince you otherwise?"

"Not a thing," Nora told him, and then turned her head slightly to press a kiss to his cheek. "You'll find I'm quite stubborn."

His eyes flickered then, with a hint of fire that made her shiver. "When this is over, and I'm not so tired, I'd like to learn more."

She laughed, and pointed to his examination room. "Go. Rest."

He was halfway there when his door opened, and Eli came inside.

Aiden seemed to come alive then, with a sudden surge of energy. "The letters! The medicine?"

"Letters delivered," Eli told him. "In two days, the medicine will be here. I was going to wait, but didn't want anyone to worry."

"That is good news," Aiden said, rubbing his hands together. "Good news indeed. Once it is here, Nora, you can help me put it into paper twists to more easily distribute."

"I've got to get home, let Hannah know I'm okay," Eli said.

"Thank you again," Aiden told the gunslinger. "I'm grateful to you."

Eli paused at the door. "I'll be here when it's delivered. We'll make sure to keep people orderly, in case word gets out."

"That's a good idea," Nora agreed.

"I'll let Gavin know too," Eli said. He waved, and then left.

Nora turned to Aiden with a smile. "This is such wonderful news!"

"It is," he agreed. He stepped closer to her. "Nora, I don't want you to think I'm not grateful for your offer. But you don't have to stay now. Two days, and we'll have the medicine. This might end soon."

She shook her head. "You can't get rid of me. I won't go."

"Perhaps then, I'll have to scare you off," Aiden said, that fire flashing in his eyes again as the room filled with an energy she couldn't explain.

Nora wasn't scared, though, and rested her hand on his arm, meeting his eyes. "Just how would you do that?"

"Kiss you," he said softly, bringing a hand to her face, "and beg you."

She tipped her head upward. "You may kiss me all you'd like," she told him, moving dangerously closer, "but I am staying to help you."

The corners of his lips turned upward, and Aiden started to pull her toward him. Nora was sure he truly was about to kiss her, when footsteps outside the door and a cry for help made him drop his hand. The disappointment in his eyes mirrored her own, but then a woman holding a limp baby opened the door.

It was time to return to reality, not the moment where she'd been nearly swept away by his touch. Nora just hoped the opportunity would return.

Chapter 14

Nora had helped him for three days there in the office. Three.

And there had been no sign of the medicine.

While Aiden was grateful for her extra pair of hands, and her ability to remain calm under pressure—like during the amputation of a gangrened toe he'd had to do that morning—his concern over the increasing number of illnesses in town grew. And without the medicine that Eli had said would be here, he was even more worried.

He'd finally gone over to the sheriff's office to ask if there was anything that could be done, but Gavin wasn't there. Impatiently, Aiden had gone back to his office, but kept one eye on the street, looking for the sheriff.

His door opened, and Nora walked in, holding several envelopes. "Mail for you," she said. "I hope you don't mind me having gotten it, but the postmaster stopped me on the way here."

"Not at all," Aiden said. "I appreciate it. Thank you."

He took the letters eagerly, hoping for good news. He was sure Nora felt the same. Quickly, Aiden scanned the bundle of letters. One was from another doctor, one from his mother, and one from his brother. He opened the one from the other doctor first.

It was short and to the point. *Yes, there is fever here. We are not faring well.*

It was not good news. Though the doctor had given no more details, Aiden understood. The man was likely as worn down as he was. He tossed the other letters onto his desk. He could deal with those later.

Aiden turned to Nora. "Did you happen to see the sheriff on your way?"

"No, but I know where he is," Nora told him. "A bull got loose over by the blacksmith. He's helping get it."

"Then I will keep watching for him," Aiden said, sitting at his desk and turning to face the window.

"I'm sure it will get here," Nora said, knowing what he meant. Of course she knew. The whole town was waiting anxiously, even if they didn't say so.

"I hope so," he answered, every bit of his body filled with tension.

"I'm going to refill your canisters of tea," Nora said, and left, holding the large sacks he'd not noticed her carrying.

That's how distracted he was. Ordinarily, he'd have jumped to help her. While the teas weren't a complete remedy, they had been able to get a substantial amount, and he was at least able to give something to patients who came in. Pastor Blackstone had also been delivering it.

Feverfew and chamomile, lavender and peppermint, he knew they had medicinal purposes, and hoped, if nothing else, to provide a placebo effect. It also would make the plain water—which Billy had been hauling to each home—taste better, had it been sitting in a pail for a day.

He'd stopped charging patients for his services. Anyone who came to him would get the help they needed, regardless of ability to pay. With only his words of comfort and tea, he felt bad at the idea of accepting payment.

There was a rustling sound from the back room, and the soothing sound of Nora humming as she worked relaxed him. She'd been a balm to his soul, and Aiden was grateful she was there with him. And more than a little thankful neither of them had gotten ill.

He eyed the letters from home, and picked up his mother's first. It was similar to most every other. She told of this bit of society news and that one, told him how his father had been, bragged about his brother, and, right at the closing paragraph, mentioned him.

Do take care of yourself out there. It's a dreadfully wild place, I hear. Not a day goes by I wish you'd stayed here. With love, Mother.

He wondered if that was true, that she wished he'd stayed. His mother had never been very affectionate toward him. Aiden put the letter in his desk drawer so he could reply later, and make mention of the things she had written, and opened his brother's letter.

It was shorter than usual.

Dear Aiden,

Since I doubt you are very needed out there, beyond snake bites and gunshots, have you been working on any research? Or do you have anything in the attic I might have? It appears that they expect me to continue to "do great things," and I have no idea what will impress them.

Since you don't need to do such a thing out there in the wilderness, do let me have it, like a decent brother.

I'll wait for your reply. Even if it's simply an ointment you've invented. I need to keep my spot here. You've endless time on your hands out there. I know you'll come through for me again. After all, we are family, and look after each other. Make it complicated. Use lots of big words when you write out how I should describe it, so I sound even better.

Phillip

Anger surged through Aiden. Endless time? Didn't he wish! He considered writing to his brother, telling him there was an epidemic sweeping through. That he was too busy saving lives to create an ointment! Fury filled each inch of him.

Spoiled. That's what his brother was.

He crumpled the letter, and threw it toward the waste bin. Phillip could wait forever. He was done helping him. His brother needed to stand on his own.

As he stood, his arm jostled the desk drawer, and his mother's letter came into view. It ruffled slightly in the breeze gently blowing in from the window, and he saw there was something written on the backside of the letter.

Aiden sat back down, and picked up the letter to turn it over. There was a short note from his father. He didn't usually write, so this was quite odd.

Son, I had a disturbing dream that you were in danger. Superstitious, perhaps, but it still concerned me. Please, for my sake, write back at once, and tell the truth if you are. Though your mother doesn't like to appear emotional, she cares for you deeply, as do I. Despite what you think, I don't have a favorite son. If there is anything at all I can do to help you in some way, I want to.

Your Father

Aiden looked at the message in surprise. While his father had said his mother didn't like to appear emotional, and it was true, he'd neglected to say that he was the same. As stoic as they came. So, to see this letter, to have that proof that his parents did care for him, in his mother's odd last paragraph and now this from his father...it was almost overwhelming.

His exhausted state didn't help, either. Aiden started to put the letter away, but a thought came to him. What if? What if he did get sick? What if something happened to him? He needed to tell his parents he cared for them as well, even if he sometimes struggled to feel that way.

Aiden reached for a sheet of paper and his pencil.

Dear Father and Mother,

I got your letter, and please let Phillip know I got his as well, but I have very little time right now. I will reply once I can.

There has been a serious epidemic that has broken out in many towns for nearly fifty miles around. Here, they call it fever and ague. Back home, you'll know it as malaria. So far, I am well, but I have treated over two hundred patients in the course of two weeks.

The danger lies not just in the virus, but also in that we don't have the medicine to treat it. I ran out some time ago. Those few who had it recovered. Those who have not... Many are fighting for their lives with nothing but tea and cool compresses.

The medicine I ordered still isn't here yet. We are all praying it comes soon. The sheriff is trying to help us obtain it.

I wish I had the energy to write you a cheerful letter. A bland letter. But I do not. I do not wish to cause you alarm by my speaking plainly, but neither did I want to miss the chance to send you one last letter, just in case.

You both have my love, and I would be humbly grateful for your prayers that the medicine arrives soon. The people of this town need it greatly. God willing, we will all be spared.

Aiden

He swallowed hard and put the letter into an envelope. "Nora, I'm going to the post office," he told her.

"It's been quiet today," Nora said brightly as she came out of the back room. "Go ahead."

What neither of them said, however, was that the quiet wasn't good. It likely meant that people were dying, and others were too weak to seek aid.

Aiden stood and went to the door. He stopped, wanting to give Nora some assurance all would be well, but he knew it would be a lie. His eyes met hers, and she gave a small nod, her sad eyes saying all he was feeling.

"I'll be back soon," he promised, and then stepped outside.

The moment he did, he tried to keep his shoulders from slumping. It wouldn't be good for anyone to see him worried. If only he could leave his worries behind him as easily as he'd closed the door.

Chapter 15

Nora's gaze followed Aiden as he left. His drooped shoulders were a combination of weariness and helplessness, she suspected. She knew that this lull in patients could only mean one thing. More were sick, and some had passed away. As empty as the town was, she knew it couldn't be because they'd recovered.

She swallowed hard, and looked about the room for something to keep her busy. When she spotted a crumpled piece of paper on the floor near the trash bin, she stooped and picked it up to drop it inside.

The handwriting wasn't familiar, and the paper—a letter, she saw—was not fully crumpled. Nora knew she shouldn't read it, but she did. Her hands shook with anger as she read Phillip's letter, and then she crumpled it herself, making sure it landed in the trash.

What a horrible man he seemed! So pompous! So spoiled! And of all the times for Aiden to have gotten this letter. Perhaps that's what had upset him. He'd gone to post something. Was it a reply to his brother? Oh, how she hoped not! Did his parents pressure him to help? She shook her head and scowled at the discarded letter.

Nora felt even worse for Aiden now. This was the last thing he needed, on top of his worries about the town's welfare. She knew she'd been right all along, about how deeply he cared for others. He'd not slept, hardly ate, and was constantly searching through his books over and over, seeking some way to help without the quinine.

She had to calm down. It would not do her any good to be this agitated, nor would it make a good impression if someone walked in, and saw her as angry as a storm. Slowly, she took in several slow, deep breaths, and let her gaze roam around the room again for a distraction.

When her eyes fell on Aiden's medical books, she picked one at random, and sat in one of the chairs usually for patients and began to read. She was so absorbed in the text, when the office door opened she startled.

Aiden smiled at her as he came through. "You must be reading something quite engrossing," he told her.

"It is," Nora said, holding up the red clothbound book.

"That old thing?" Aiden laughed as he stood next to her. "It's so old, the name is worn off, but one of my professors gave it to me in medical school. It was his father's. It must be fifty years old. The information is still quite good for many things, however. While medical advancements have come a long way since this was first printed, some things, like human anatomy, have not."

"I enjoyed my uncle's books as well," Nora said. "I find the medical field fascinating."

She wondered, as those words sparked a sudden idea, if this might be a path for her. The way forward with her life, as a nurse. Maybe not any nurse, but Aiden's. She'd like to ask if he'd teach her more, but this wasn't the time.

Heavy footsteps came outside the door, and Nora and Aiden traded the look they'd begun to share. Part fear, part dread, part resignation.

Pastor Blackstone entered. When he spotted them, he removed the small hat from his head. "Doctor, I needed to let you know. Billy and I were visiting families this afternoon. We've found two dead today. Part of the Roberts family. Quite a few others are very weak. Might not make it."

"Oh no," Nora whispered, her hands flying to her lips. The Roberts had come in a few days before, with all of them feeling poorly. They were a family of seven, the oldest child nine, the youngest but a few weeks. She didn't ask which of the family had died. She didn't want to know.

"I've got to make the sheriff aware," the pastor said. He turned to leave, but then stopped, as though he were going to say something.

Nora stood, watching him, but he simply sighed and left. She turned to Aiden. "The Roberts," she whispered. "They were just here."

He nodded, and closed his eyes for a moment, then ran his hands over his face. "You should go home. Things will get worse. But if you leave now, you won't have to hear more."

"Why are you saying that?" Nora asked.

Aiden looked at her, pain in his eyes. "I warned you. This is why I didn't want you here, yet selfishly I let you stay because I like being with you. I don't want you to suffer, to have doubts if you've done enough."

"You didn't *let* me do anything. I chose to stay. I knew the risks, and I accepted them willingly." Nora crossed her arms. "I'm quite capable of making my own decisions."

"You are also so stubborn," Aiden told her. He sighed. "I don't mean to sound angry. It's just you were here for a trip. To enjoy yourself. Not be cooped up in a doctor's office, attending a widespread outbreak of malaria."

She shrugged. "It will make for an interesting story later. Unlike the wounds on my face would have."

"But when you leave, you don't need to go with these kinds of memories," he told her, nearly pleading.

"I haven't decided I am going to leave," Nora said, raising her chin. "I might stay forever. I have reason to."

He closed his eyes again. "I see why your brother looks frustrated at times."

She threw her arms in the air. "I can't help it. I've always been this way. If I see something I want, I go after it. And that's why I'm staying. Staying right here in your office and, I hope, staying in Red Ridge."

Aiden blinked several times and looked around, bewildered. "What on earth could you possibly see in this office that you want?"

She laughed, and stepped closer. The confused look on his face made her love him even more. "You. You foolish man. I said before I was falling for you. That hasn't changed. What's happening in the town doesn't change that either.

"I know the risks, and I don't plan to leave. I don't plan to leave you, and I don't plan to leave this town. Not unless it's abundantly clear that you feel nothing for me. Because if you do, if one of us is to perish, I've decided that I want to know that I spent my final days experiencing love. But not just any love. Your love."

Chapter 16

Aiden knew the moment was here. He needed to reply. He needed to tell her what was in his heart and on his mind as well. He couldn't delay. No matter this wasn't really the time, Nora had made it such.

And could he blame her, considering the circumstances? No, he couldn't. In truth, she was right. Just as he'd felt compelled to write his parents one last time, just in case, he knew Nora was right in telling him how she felt.

Just in case.

He prayed it wouldn't come to that. That fate, having finally allowed them to meet, to love, would not separate them. But sometimes, one didn't have a choice. As had happened with the Roberts family. Days, hours, years...all were limited. It was foolish to waste them.

He'd spent so many moments thinking about her, imagining himself with her beyond these office walls. Wondering if she truly cared for him as much as he'd hoped. Yet, he knew it was impossible. They were impossible.

"Nora," he said with a sigh, as he took her hands in his. "I don't know what to say."

"Something in reply to what I said would be wise," Nora said, a hint of sarcasm in her voice. "Here, I've poured my heart out to you."

"I know," Aiden whispered. "And I want your love. I want to give you mine."

"Then what is holding you back?" Nora asked, searching his face. "I know these are serious times, but why do you look more concerned than I'd think someone would after hearing that?

He wasn't sure if he should tell her, but the way she was looking at him, a mixture of pain and desperation filling her lovely face, the words dragged themselves out of him before he'd realized it.

"I'm a simple doctor. I'll never be rich, and give you the things you are used to. I'm not the right one for you, Nora. I can't give a woman like you the life you deserve. I've been selfish keeping you here for my pleasure, entertaining thoughts of something more with you."

Confusion flickered over her. "What do you think I deserve?"

"Everything," Aiden told her. "A large home, a full staff, all the dresses you could long for. Parties and, and...and all of the things you likely have always had. Your father was a businessman, and I assume quite wealthy, since you traveled so much for him."

"I have never had those things," Nora told him gently. "Except for the large house. There were so many of us we had to have one. I think you have this misconception that our family was—is—well off. That's not the case."

"Perhaps not," he stammered, feeling as though he'd made a fool of himself, "but—"

"Those things you listed, those aren't what I want. I want a home I can feel happy and content in. I am not worried about having a staff that I must pay and oversee. That sounds a good deal of work. As for dresses, I don't need a large number of them. Parties, well, I'm a quiet sort. I do enjoy when Billy has his friends over, but I find I often seek the corners of the room, and have more pleasure watching than partaking.

"But you've not mentioned the things that I do want. All I want is happiness and to feel a sense of belonging. I feel those things with you, Aiden. Though I've traveled a good deal on Father's behalf, and I've met many people, I've never met someone like you. Someone who my heart instantly pulls me to. The person who I can't stop thinking about, at any time of day."

"I am nearly speechless," Aiden said softly. "I ask your forgiveness for making assumptions."

"Why did you?" Nora asked, tilting her head slightly. "I do hope I've not put on airs, and made you think I was more than I appeared."

"That's not it," he assured her. "I think...you see, my family was quite critical of my coming here. Just before I left, I overheard my mother and my brother talking about me. They were both in agreement that this would be the best I could ever have. A sleepy town in the middle of nowhere. I wasn't cut out for a position such as he held."

The fire in Nora's eyes warmed his heart, and made him love her all the more.

"How terrible of them," she said. Then, she lowered her head. "I must apologize and also be truthful with you. I saw his recent letter to you. It was on the floor. As I was throwing it away, I read it. I know I had no right. It was personal, and I hope you'll forgive me."

Aiden winced. "Yes. Phillip's letter. I'm quite used to those. It was a relief moving away from that in-person commentary. I don't know what I've done in my life to make my brother be so against me."

"I can only imagine the relief that miles must bring," Nora said. "But I want you to know that they are quite wrong. This town needs you. It's not a sleepy town where nothing happens." She laughed softly. "Trouble seems to find Red Ridge as quickly as a child does a cookie in the kitchen. Things might have started slowly for you, but I'd say they've more than made up for that, these last few weeks."

"You've got that right," Aiden agreed.

"But there's something else we didn't finish discussing, and that's the possibility of us. If you don't want such a thing, then please tell me," Nora said. "Don't worry about hurting my feelings. I'd rather know, than be made a fool of."

Aiden's chest felt tight, and he shook his head. "Nora," he whispered, bringing his hands to her face, "I will never not want you. For as long as I live, you will always be the first thing on my mind each morning, and the last before I sleep, until dreams take over and you are there as well. I want you. I want us."

"That makes me happier than you can possibly know," Nora said.

"When this fever and ague leaves, I want to spend time with you, beyond these walls, and tell you all of the words that have been stored up within me. To let you know just how much I care for you," Aiden said.

"I would like that very much, and I cannot wait for that day," Nora whispered.

Aiden brought his lips to hers, but just as they brushed against her own, his office door flung open, and he and Nora startled away.

A young woman he didn't recognize stood there, panic in her eyes. When she caught sight of Nora, she rushed over to her.

"You must help me!" she cried out.

"Callie, what is wrong?" Nora asked.

"My husband! I think he's dying."

Chapter 17

Callie fell against Nora. "He won't drink or eat. He's been in bed for days with a fever. It has him delirious," the woman said through her sobs. "You must have something you can do to help!"

"I can give you some teas," Aiden said, coming over soothingly. "Medicines should be arriving any day. I'll be sure some are taken to you, Mrs—"

The door opened, and Billy walked in. He took one look at Callie and asked, "What's going on?"

"George is dying," Callie said, grabbing his arm. "There's no medicine."

Billy's face turned dark before he quickly smoothed it. "It's on its way," he promised her. "The moment we've got it, I'll send some right over. I promise."

Callie nodded as she wiped at her eyes. "I'm sorry, Billy. I just...I'm scared."

"I understand," Nora said, wrapping her arm around her. "I will make you up those teas, with the doctor's permission?"

"Of course," Aiden said. "Nora, package up some of the chamomile and the feverfew."

"Right away," Nora said. She hurried to the back room and scooped the dried leaves into paper twists. When she returned, she said to Callie, "You can drink the chamomile yourself. Might help."

"Thank you," Callie said, squaring her shoulders. "I apologize."

"Don't," Nora said. "I'll let Mirabelle know. Maybe she can stop over."

Callie nodded and left. The moment the door closed, Billy smacked one fist into the palm of his other hand. "We've got to do something! Where's that medicine?"

The door opened just as he asked. Nora stepped back slightly, to allow the newcomers room to enter. With an angry look on his face, Gavin answered his friend's question. "Someone's been hoarding it. Charging four times the price. Not a speck to be found anywhere but from them, my friend says."

"What?" Nora gasped. "That's not right!"

"Maybe not," Eli said quietly, "but some folks don't care. Truth be told," he added, "I don't either. We'll buy it. Lives are more precious than dollars."

"I don't know how much money I have," Aiden said. "And I can't pass along that exorbitant price to the town. I promised not to charge for this."

"No need to," Eli said calmly. "I said *we'd* buy it. I meant me, Billy, and Gavin. We've enough it won't even make a dent in our bank accounts."

Aiden frowned. "I don't think I like that idea. I am the town doctor. You must let me contribute. "

"You already are, by not charging anyone," Billy said.

Gavin nodded. "We will settle up later if we need to. But first, we've got to get it."

"I'll go," Billy offered. "In fact, I'll take Nick with me. Then it won't be as scary-like, a bunch of men coming in and asking questions. Less likely to get attacked too. Just a couple of brothers out and doing brotherly things."

"That's a good idea," Gavin said. "Not sure Winnie will approve completely of you taking her brother with you, but under the circumstances...and the kid's good backup."

"What can I do to help?" Nora asked.

"Since we know the medicine will be here soon," Aiden started.

"In about six hours, if we leave right quick," Billy interrupted.

"Then, Nora, I'd be grateful if you helped me prepare the paper into cones. Then, once the medicine is here, we can scoop it in them faster. It could potentially be delivered tonight, even if it's dark out."

"I can do that," Nora agreed. She put a hand on her brother's arm. "I know you have to get Nick before you leave. Please, stop and tell me before you leave town."

"I will," he said, and turned to leave, hurrying out with Gavin.

Nora closed her eyes for a moment. "I pray they get it," she said.

"I've the feeling if anyone can, it will be them," Aiden said.

"I agree," Nora said. "Let's prepare the paper cones."

Aiden went into his examination room, where he kept them stored. A second later, there was a crash. "Oh no!" his voice cried from the back.

"What is it?" Nora asked.

"I knocked over the wash water, and it soaked them. I have more paper, but we'll have to cut it."

"Then that will give us something to do," Nora said calmly. "Bring it here, and we will do it at your desk."

They worked quietly. About a half hour later, the sound of horses made Nora look up, and she opened the office door, stepping outside. Aiden followed her.

Billy jumped down from his horse. "Wanted to fully gear up," he said, "but that might be too obvious." He patted his gun holster. "Only taking two."

Her eyes went to Nick, who was grinning wide. "I can't believe it! Off on a gunslinger mission," he said eagerly.

"It's serious work," Billy reminded him. "And you can't get hurt. Or else Winnie might hurt me."

"Yeah, she would," Nick agreed with a laugh. "She's right scary with a rolling pin."

"Be safe," Nora said, and kissed her brother's cheek. "I'm not leaving here until you are back."

Her brother nodded, and swung back on his horse. He and Nick rode quickly, and dust kicked up behind them. Faintly, she could see the empty saddlebags bouncing. Soon, they'd be filled with life-saving medicines.

Nora watched until they were out of sight. An arm slipped around her shoulders, and Aiden gently squeezed, before releasing her. "He'll be okay," he assured her.

She smiled at him, wishing that he hadn't moved his arm. Wishing he'd put it back there again soon.

They returned to cutting the paper and twisting it into shape to speed up the medicine distribution. Nora's head began to ache, and she felt a terrible thirst. After her third cup of water, she realized she felt warm, and her body was starting to ache.

She glanced at Aiden's examination room. He was with a patient right now. She moved closer to the window, seeking the breeze, and drank another cup of water.

She couldn't be sick. She wouldn't let herself be. This was just fatigue from working so hard. That was all. The headache from the stress.

"And keep off that foot, Mrs. Davis," Aiden said as he helped the older woman out to her wagon. "I'll see you next week to look at it again."

A few moments later, he sank down at his desk. "How nice it is to have a patient without a fever," he said with a small laugh.

"Indeed," Nora said, hoping she didn't look flushed.

"If I ever complain about being bored with my patient load, please, give me one of those glares you give your brother."

Nora laughed. "I promise." She stood up and stretched, then said, "My back is aching from being bent over so long. Do you mind if I step out for a few moments? I'll return these dishes to Madge."

"Go ahead," Aiden said. "You more than deserve a break. I wonder if she has any pie left."

"I'll ask," Nora said. "That does sound good."

Nora took up the tray their dinner had been brought on and stepped outside. The cool air helped tremendously, and she felt a little better. Surely, she wasn't coming down with the fever and ague.

Nora returned the dishes and tray, was delighted to accept two slices of strawberry cake from Lisa, then slowly walked back to the doctor's office. It would be sunset soon. The sun was lowering, and the sky was turning a brilliant shade of red and orange.

She'd just stepped back into the office and set the cake on Aiden's desk when the sound of horses racing toward them filled her ears. Nora turned and rushed to the front of the building, staggering a little in her weariness. Thankfully, Aiden hadn't noticed. He was focused on the riders.

Gavin was hurrying over from across the street. As the horses pulled up, Billy's face was the angriest she'd ever seen it in her life. Even Nick, so like him and always quick to laugh or make a joke, looked furious.

"What's wrong?" Nora asked her brother.

He met her eyes solemnly. "The medicine has been stolen."

Chapter 18

Stolen. The medicine was stolen. Who could have done such a thing? Didn't they realize that the lives of many depended on it?

Aiden was sure in that moment that the anger flooding his veins matched that of Nora's, who was standing there, her hands balled into fists. He might have smiled, were this not so serious, at how her face nearly matched her brother's.

"Only one thing for it," Gavin said, and pulled one of his revolvers out of his gun belt, checking his bullets. "Nick, you get on home to your sister."

"I'm going with you," the teenager said stubbornly. "The town needs all of us."

"Wait, what's going on?" Aiden asked, perplexed by the sudden exchange.

"I'll get the rifles," Eli said, appearing at his side. "Billy, you get fresh horses for us."

Aiden startled. Where had the other gunslinger come from? "Rifles? Fresh horses? Will one of you explain to me what's happening? I thought the medicine was stolen. You look like you are..." His eyes widened.

"That's right, we're about to go get it," Billy said. "Don't you worry. You'll get that medicine." The hardness in his eyes was terrifying, and Aiden was glad it wasn't directed toward him.

Gavin was checking his gun, and Eli coming back over from the sheriff's office with rifles.

"Take me with you," Aiden said. The firmness in his voice surprised him. The squinting looks of doubt and surprise from the gunslingers and their young protégé, however, did not.

"Why?" Billy asked.

"Because if you are going to go to all the trouble of tracking down the people who stole it, you'd best have someone there who can identify you're getting the right medicine, and not some snake oil concoction," Aiden said. "We'd be in even worse condition if that happened.

"Sounds reasonable," Eli said with a shrug. "I say let the doc come."

"Get him a horse too," Gavin ordered Billy.

Nora's brother vanished. Aiden felt a hand on his arm and turned to Nora, who was looking at him with fear in her eyes. "Aiden," she whispered.

He swallowed. "I'll be fine. Really."

She gave him a tiny smile. "What a story this will be for your family when you write them next."

"Don't worry, we'll keep him safe," Billy said, reappearing, another horse at the ready.

The others nodded, and Aiden took a deep breath. "Right, then."

The next few moments were a whirlwind. He didn't have time to give Nora a proper goodbye, and that ate at him as he rode hard with the gunslingers, grateful his horse could keep up with little effort on his behalf.

"Was told Ryan tracked him to a shack in the woods," Billy called to the others.

"Ryan's around?" Eli asked.

"Yeah," Billy said. "Just so happened to run into him. Once he's done with whatever he was doing, says he has a job out this way."

"Well now, if Ryan Lundy says something's so, it's so," Gavin said. "Feeling more optimistic already."

Aiden wanted to ask who this Ryan Lundy was, but was too busy trying to stay seated on his horse. He'd never ridden this fast in his life, and was sure he never wanted to again. He wasn't worried so much about the horse keeping up—it was neck and neck. No, he was worried about falling, and breaking his own neck at this pace.

"About twenty miles that way," Billy said, pointing, and the horses followed.

Nick rode close to Aiden. The teenager looked a mixture of serious and excited. He supposed at his age, he might have been the same if the men he spent time with had been gunslingers, and he were invited along to a possible shootout.

Aiden suddenly sat a little taller. He *was* along with them. Holding his own as well! And Nora was right. This would be quite a story to tell his family. He could almost imagine Phillip's expression. It was enough to make Aiden smile. He just needed to make sure this tale ended well.

They rode until the sky was black. The horses almost seemed to know the way, and Billy rode in the lead. As they slowed in a thickly wooded area, Aiden's horse started to nicker and move restlessly.

Billy rode near him, whispering something. The horse instantly behaved.

"Impressive," Aiden said. "Whatever you did."

"He's our horse whisperer," Eli said. "Can tame most any animal."

"Shhh," Gavin warned. "Dismount."

They climbed off their horses and tied them to trees.

"We'll go on foot," Eli said. "Standard pattern, spaced."

"What does that mean?" Aiden whispered.

"That means they go ahead, and you and I got to stay behind," Nick muttered.

"You're a bodyguard," Gavin said, putting a hand on the teenager's shoulder. "Not second class. Someone's got to watch the doc. Bet he don't have a gun. Something happens to him, none of us know how to dose this medicine. He's important. So is your job."

Nick seemed to stand a little taller at those words. "No one's gonna hurt him," he promised.

The gunslingers crept forward, splitting up. There was a partial moon, enough that Aiden could make out their stealthy movements, since his eyes had adjusted. He walked forward as well, though he made sure to stay at least a dozen paces behind.

Close to him, Nick was stone-faced. His eyes scanned the area, reminding Aiden of a younger version of each of the men he could see before him. He had no doubt the young man would grow to be every bit as protective of Red Ridge as the others were.

The cabin about twenty paces away was lit up from the inside, and light seeped through the cracks. Aiden strained his ears to hear something from within, but he was too far away.

Billy had put himself at one window. It looked like Gavin had moved around the other side, and Eli had positioned himself near the door.

Aiden and Nick moved closer, stopping at a wide tree that gave good cover. Faint voices drifted in the air.

"Gonna be rich! Rich I tell you!" someone hooted.

"Can't wait to meet with Bobby Jim tomorrow. Get our reward," another said. "How much you reckon we got?"

"Don't know. Got a lock on the box," the first said. "Gimmie yer knife to break it."

"I'm not giving you my knife! You'll bust it up. Use yours."

"Can't. Already busted it," the other man said, his voice mournful.

"What do you think they'll do?" Aiden asked Nick softly.

"I figure they'll either bust open the doors at the same time, or else knock, see if they can get them to come out," Nick answered, never taking his eyes from the scene before them.

"How would they know to bust in at the same time?" Aiden asked.

"I dunno. They just do. They've worked together so long, they just...read minds or something. When me and Lily were kidnapped, and Gavin came to rescue us, they showed up just in the nick of time as the saloon owner was about to shove Winnie out the upstairs window."

"What?" Aiden stared at the young man. "I have missed out on a lot of stories, it seems. Does Eli's wife have one too?"

"Sure does," Nick said. He flashed a grin at Aiden before he turned his attention back to the cabin. "Stick around, Doc, and maybe you'll get your own story folks'll tell about you. These guys have a million. Done a lot."

"It would seem," Aiden murmured.

A low whistle filled his ears, then the hooting of an owl. Another owl answered, and there was a loud crash, as the cabin doors were kicked in. At least, Aiden assumed both were, by the loud noise. He was also assuming the owl hoots hadn't been owls.

Shots rang out, and Nick and Aiden started running. Aiden wasn't sure what he could do without a weapon, but he'd figure that out when he got there.

Just as he reached the porch, a shot whizzed past him. He knocked Nick to the ground as a second bullet hit the porch post, an inch away from where Nick's head had been.

"Woo wee," Nick hollered as he scrambled to his feet. "Thanks, Doc!"

There was scuffling inside, and Aiden rose to his hands and knees, trying to see better as he scrambled upright.

"We give up! We give up!" a man screeched.

"Don't kill us!" the other howled.

Aiden entered the cabin as Gavin was hauling one man to a chair, and Eli to another. In short work, the two men—both perhaps in their forties, with a rank odor and few teeth—were bound to the wooden chairs.

"This is it," Billy said, looking over his shoulder at Aiden. "I was told the medicines were in a wooden chest."

"Medicines?" one of the men said. "That ain't no medicine! That there is gold!"

"Who told you that?" Billy asked.

The man shrugged. "The way it was locked, that's what did." He smirked. "You ain't real smart."

"Did it never occur to you that gold is heavy?" Eli asked. "And this box, filled to the brim with gold, would be more than one of you, perhaps even both of you, could carry?"

The thieves traded glances. Finally, one said sheepishly, "Didn't think of that."

"I imagine not," Gavin said dryly. "Let's open it."

Billy reached for his gun, Aiden was assuming, to shoot off the lock. "Stop!" Aiden shouted. "I do not have the time to separate shards of glass from the medicine."

Nick plucked a knife off the ground. "I'll pop it open," he said.

"That's my knife!" one of the thieves whined.

Aiden glared at him, and the man quieted. Nick had the lock open in short order, and Aiden quickly inspected the large wooden box's contents. The glass jars were intact, and he opened them, smelling each.

"This is it," he told them, relief filling his every pore. "It's the quinine."

"Let's get it back," Billy said.

"I'll take these two," Gavin said calmly. "Nick? Give me a hand?"

"Yes, sir," Nick said.

"We'll get this back to town," Eli said. "Good work, men."

"Indeed," Aiden said, helping to secure the box to his horse.

Billy mounted, and he, Eli, and Aiden rode back to Red Ridge. Aiden should have felt tired, but instead he was elated. They had the medicine. They were also uninjured. It had been a good adventure, but he would be quite satisfied, thinking back to it, not going on another.

"By the time we get there, sun will be up," Eli said. "Can get right to work passing it out."

"I just pray it's not too late," Aiden said quietly, mentally counting how many they needed to treat.

The gunslingers didn't say anything, but he knew they were praying for the same.

Chapter 19

Mirabelle walked into the doctor's office. Nora stood, then grabbed onto the back of the chair for support. She'd been dozing. It was just she was overtired, that was all.

"Is everything all right?" Nora asked anxiously.

Her sister-in-law studied her. "I am wondering the same about you." Mirabelle put her hand on Nora's forehead. "You are blazing."

"It's just hot, that's all," Nora said, reaching for her tea to ease her parched throat. "No word yet from the others. I hope they'll be back soon."

"I have bad news," Mirabelle said, her voice low.

Nora gave Mirabelle her full attention. At least, as much as she could with the endless throbbing in her head.

"Callie came to the house." Mirabelle twisted her hands.

"How is she? Her husband?" Nora asked. She sat back down. She was so tired. Standing was becoming more and more difficult.

"He's dead."

Nora's eyes shot to Mirabelle, and she felt speechless.

"She's in shock, I think. She didn't know what to do. I told her...I told her I'd come to town and get Papa to take care of everything."

"That's a good idea," Nora said slowly, feeling numbness from the shock herself. She dropped her head into her hands. "Aiden didn't want me here because of this."

"The sickness?" Mirabelle asked.

"No, well, yes, but also he wasn't sure how I'd be able to handle it when patients died. Especially if I knew them."

Mirabelle was quiet, then she said, "I don't know how anyone can handle any sort of tragedy, other than to keep moving forward. As a pastor's daughter, I've experienced the loss of several of the churchgoers over the years. Those I knew well, those I didn't."

"It's a hard thing to lose someone, especially the ones you knew well." Nora recalled her uncle and aunt talking about how they'd often had trouble sleeping, wondering if they could have done more. Was that something Aiden ever did? She couldn't ask him, and she had no experience herself, but she could ask her friend. "Did their faces stay with you in nightmares?"

Mirabelle took a moment to think before she answered. "Remembering them, and sharing their memories with others, and feeling blessed for the time we got to spend together is what Papa told us to do. It's hard, though. I won't lie. I keep thinking, were it Callie, how devastated I'd be. Would I ever stop being sad? What if something happened to Billy? Mama? Papa? How could I keep going?

"But I think, perhaps, it's also a little like when you have to say goodbye to a friend because you are moving away. You'll see them again one day. Maybe not on earth, but up in heaven. So, the loss, and the pain of the parting, it *is* hard. I think, though, I'd rather have that pain because it meant I knew them, loved them, than to never experience that. Even if I never got a proper chance to say goodbye, and I might have regrets."

"That's a wonderful way to look at it," Nora said. "I have no regrets being here. I just pray none of my efforts have been futile."

"They have not," Mirabelle assured her. Then she gasped. "I think it's them!"

Nora struggled to stand, but managed to walk toward the door. Her eyes felt blurred, and her whole body on fire. She blinked several times, hoping to clear her vision.

Distantly, she could hear voices, but everything began to swim, suddenly, and dim. The last thing she recalled was falling, falling, and then stopping, as something held her close.

An unfamiliar smell, one of horses and sweat, was in her nostrils, and that was the last thing Nora remembered.

***

"Nora?"

On the cool pillow, Nora stirred slightly. Every movement was difficult. Tiring. She tried to speak. She was sure her lips moved, but nothing came out.

"Give me the tea," another voice said. She wasn't sure who. Her ears felt muffled.

Cool liquid dribbled into her mouth, and Nora drank eagerly. The tea seemed to give her energy, and she managed to crack her eyes open.

Winnie was there, and Mirabelle.

"I'm here too," Hannah called. "But the doctor won't let me in to see you. Not until he's sure the fever's broken."

"I'll have Gus ride for him," Mirabelle said, hurrying out of the room.

Nora closed her eyes for a moment, but she must have fallen asleep. Someone's hand on her wrist woke her, and her eyes fluttered as her vision cleared. It was a relief to be able to see clearly again.

"Aiden?" she whispered.

His usually composed face was anguished. "Nora," he whispered, bringing his hands to her face to cup her cheeks. "I was so worried."

"I'm fine," she told him. "I was just tired. That's all."

"No, you were very ill," he said.

Though she was still tired, the tiniest of smiles worked its way to Nora's lips. "Are you really here? Or am I dreaming?" she asked.

"I'm here." Aiden took one of her hands in his and kissed her palm.

She was able to hear better. It seemed her entire body was waking, after being in this bed for who knew how long. Footsteps in the hallway drew closer, and Nora turned her head to see Billy standing there, his cheeks damp.

"You scared me," he scolded her, voice cracking as he wrapped her in a hug. "How was I going to tell Ma?"

"Can't have that," Nora teased, though her voice sounded weak, even to her ears. "And I told you I wouldn't let it happen. Here I am, fine and healthy." She glanced at Aiden then. "I am, aren't I?"

"Yes," he assured her. "Now that the fever is broken, you should recover swiftly. I prescribe a few more days of bedrest, and as much food or drink as you feel you can tolerate."

"Bedrest?" Nora argued. "I am able to get back to work."

"Not yet," Aiden told her. He stood, looking regretful. "I dislike leaving, but I need to go check on a few more people. I will return tomorrow to look in on you."

He left, and Nora's eyes followed him as long as they could. Mirabelle settled next to her, and Nora turned her attention toward her. "What did I miss?" she asked. "How long have I been in bed?"

"Three days," Mirabelle told her. "Let's see. As Billy, Eli, and Aiden were riding up, you and I went to greet them. You collapsed, however, and I'm not sure how he did it, but Aiden nearly threw himself under you to keep you from hitting the ground. He managed to break your fall, and then we brought you here."

"I think I remember falling," Nora said. "Everything went black. So, I've been here for three days." She shook her head slowly. "I don't remember anything else until I woke up."

"The medicine was distributed," Mirabelle continued. "Every able-bodied person worked together. There was enough, and a little extra to have on hand, but also to offer to another town if needed. A good number have recovered fully, and quite a few are like you, starting to recover."

"What of losses?" Nora asked. "I remember you told me about Callie's husband. Were there more?"

"Thirty in all, Papa says," Mirabelle said quietly. "It could have been so much worse, had we no doctor here, and had he and the others not been able to procure the medicine."

Nora swallowed. Thirty. In a town this size, that had to mean almost no family was spared. Her eyes closed for a moment, and she gave a silent prayer for the comfort of their living loved ones.

"I agree. We are fortunate to have a doctor who worked so hard to get the medicine, and our gunslingers, who helped locate it," Nora said.

"You should rest," Mirabelle said. "I'll come back later."

"That's all I've done for days," Nora sighed. "I'm sure I couldn't sleep another hour."

"The sooner you heal, the sooner you can get up," her sister-in-law replied.

"Fine, fine," Nora sighed.

She let Mirabelle adjust her pillows and then lay back, intending to stare out the window and wish she were anywhere but in bed, but the moment her head touched the cool pillow, her eyes grew heavy, and she fell asleep.

The next time Nora woke, her eyes fell on Aiden.

"Hello," she whispered. "Is it tomorrow?"

"Hello," he said, reaching over and taking her hand. "It is. How are you feeling?"

Nora took a moment to consider the question. "Better," she finally said.

"Good." He listened to her heart, examined her throat and eyes, and nodded in satisfaction. "You are on the mend. I'm glad of that."

"So am I. I'm just sorry I became ill and worried you."

"You had us all worried," Aiden said. He took her hand again. "I don't know what I would do without you."

She smiled. "It feels nice to hear you say that." Then, something came to mind.

"Have you written to your family? They will likely be anxious for another letter."

"No, but I ought to," Aiden agreed. "You are right. I suppose even if I often doubted their concern or affection, it might have just been hidden."

"I expect your news will give your parents something to talk about for quite a while. What happened when you went to get the medicine? No one has told me yet," Nora asked.

Aiden shook his head. "I still can't believe it myself."

He told her about the ride through the darkness, how the gunslingers had worked in perfect synchronization, the bullet that had nearly struck Nick's head, and how when the thieves were caught, they'd foolishly thought the medicines were gold.

As he recounted the story, Nora's eyes were wide, she was sure, and she could hardly keep from gasping at some points. At the story's end, she shook her head. "My goodness. That is quite a story. I'm grateful it had a happy ending. That is a little too much adventure for my liking."

"Mine too," Aiden admitted. "But I had to go."

"You did," Nora said. "So be sure to include that in the letter too. You saved the entire town. Had you not been here, many more—if not all—of us could have perished. I've never been so proud of any man."

"Then that makes my surprise for you even better, perhaps," Aiden said.

It was only then she noticed he was holding a small brown paper-wrapped object on his lap. "What is that?" Nora asked.

"It's for you," Aiden told her. "It's a thank you for helping me. I know it's not likely appropriate, but I bought you something. It also can be a get-well gift, something to entertain you a little while you are in bed."

"You didn't have to!" Nora said as she accepted the bundle.

He shrugged. "It's small. But, perhaps when you use it, if you do, you'll think of me."

Nora's lips curved into a smile. "Many things make me think of you. I'm delighted to have another now. And, one that is from you."

Carefully, she undid the twine around the paper and watched as the wrapping fell away from a beautiful dark blue book. She flipped through it, delighted to see it was blank on the inside.

"I thought you might like to write your experiences in there," he told her. "Of your time in Red Ridge while you were here. So that if the time comes you must leave..." He stopped, and Nora hugged the book to her chest.

"I will cherish this always. As for leaving...I rather thought I'd stay. Since there seemed to be something—someone—to stay for?"

Aiden brought a hand to her cheek. "I would love it if you did," he said softly. "I hope you don't mind, but I also inscribed the book to you."

She gasped, and opened the first page. "To Nora, who I one day hope to call my own."

Chapter 20

"Good morning, Doctor!" a woman greeted as Aiden strode down the street.

"Good morning," he replied with a nod.

"Mornin', Doc," a man said as he walked past.

"How's that arm?" Aiden called.

"Right as a blue sky!" the man answered, waving it in the air.

"Doc," Old Gus said, as he waved from the general store.

"What's the weather today?" Aiden asked.

Gus tapped his weather knee—more accurate than any almanac, everyone said—and answered, "Nice until evening. Then a storm."

"Much obliged," Aiden said, and continued on his way.

A moment later, Aiden approached his office door and unlocked it, remarking on how much lighter he felt here as Red Ridge's doctor. It had only taken a wide-sweeping illness to make him feel useful and as if he belonged.

But now that he did, he was in no hurry to ever go through something like that again.

With a quick glance around to ensure everything was ready for the day, Aiden sat behind his desk and pulled out a sheet of paper. It was time to answer his brother's letter he'd sent just before all of this started.

His parents had been most relieved to get his second letter, and had told him, for likely the first time he'd recalled in a long time, just how proud they were of him. His mother had gone so far as to say she knew she'd made the right choice, sacrificing her son so that he could save the lives of hundreds.

Aiden had laughed softly as he read that part. He thought Nora might be right, that his mother would go around telling everyone what had happened. Including the part about joining the gunslingers to track down the stolen medicine.

He reached for his pen and thought for a moment before writing.

Dear Phillip,

Sorry I've been unable to write before now. I'm sure Mother and Father told you, an epidemic swept the town and the surrounding areas, and I had to go after the medicine when it was stolen by thieves. Just a day's work here in the West.

Aiden sighed, crumpled the letter, and threw it in the trash. He couldn't do it. Bragging was his brother's area. Not his. So, he began again.

Dear Phillip,

I'm sorry it has taken me so long to reply to you. You'd asked about an ointment, or something else for research. I'm afraid I have none, but I also think you don't need one. You are a clever individual, and I have every confidence you will be able to create just what they are looking for.

Might I even offer the idea of research into more malaria treatments? It is sorely needed throughout the States, and so many lives depend on it.

I hope you'll be able to visit one day. We've a curious collection of people in this growing town, but each one of them would give up their dollars or their lives to help another here. It's a most refreshing thing, really, and I'm settling in quite nicely and proud to call Red Ridge home. There's also someone I'd like you all to meet one day.

I'm afraid this is short, but my office is about to open, and I see a few people waiting for me.

Until next time,

Aiden

His door opened just as he folded the letter, and he smiled as Nora walked in. She headed straight toward him and glanced at the letter.

"Oh! To Phillip?" she asked.

"Yes. Unfortunately for him, he'll have to do his own research, but I did invite him to come here one day."

"I wonder if he will," Nora said, settling in at a small desk near his.

"I doubt it, but I've offered." Aiden shrugged.

His eyes followed Nora as she pulled out the day's schedule. Two weeks after she'd recovered, he allowed her to come in twice a week to assist him. She was now here three days a week. The number of days suited her, and him. He enjoyed her company and missed when she wasn't here. The office felt far emptier.

Perhaps it also was. Patients tended to come in heavier the days that she was there, and she was wonderful with the children. The women also seemed more comfortable with her, and would often relay sensitive information to her that she would relay to him, in order to treat them.

Things were falling into place.

There was just one more thing he needed to do, to really ensure it.

"Nora," Aiden said, "I'd like to take you to lunch today. Will you join me?"

"I would love to," she answered. "Is there a special occasion?"

"Every day with you is special," he told her honestly.

Her soft laughter filled his ears, and put a smile on his face that was still there when the next patient came in.

Over the next few hours, he and Nora tended to a broken arm, a head wound, sores that weren't healing, and a rash. As the last patient left, he turned the sign on his door to Out to Lunch and offered his arm to Nora.

Together, they strolled slowly toward the diner. Nora's face was tipped up to the sunshine, and she sighed softly. "What a beautiful day."

"I'm glad I get to spend it with you," Aiden told her as he opened the diner door.

They went inside, and Madge greeted them. "What can I get you?" she asked.

"I would like the gravy dumplings," Nora said.

"Could I have the pot roast?" Aiden requested.

"Out in a few," the woman said, and vanished into the kitchen.

Once she was gone, he carefully drank a sip of his water, and then moved the cup twice from where he'd put it. He nudged the fork and knife, then adjusted his napkin before he realized he was fidgeting.

"Is something wrong?" Nora asked, a little concern in her voice. "You seem...apprehensive."

"I have to ask you something," Aiden told her, "and I'm not sure how."

"Ah," Nora said with a nod. "Have you tried talking? I find that usually works well when I want to ask something."

He laughed at her hint of sarcasm, and then nodded his thanks as Madge set their meals in front of them.

"Anything else?" the woman asked.

"Not just yet," Aiden said. "But I'm thinking we will want some of that carrot cake on your menu."

"Yes, we will!" Nora said.

"I'll be sure to bring it out," the woman said with a wink as she walked over to another table.

Aiden and Nora ate for a few moments in silence, and then Aiden sighed. How was he to ask this? It was too serious to make a mistake on. Nora was too important to upset. He frowned and stabbed one of his fried potatoes. How did one start this sort of conversation?

"That poor potato," Nora said teasingly.

"I wanted to make sure it didn't fall off," he said with a raised brow.

Her only answer was laughter.

Aiden sighed. "I have to ask a question. But if I mess up too terribly, please take pity on me, and give me a chance to rectify the situation."

"I might," Nora agreed.

"Thank y—wait! What do you mean, you might?"

"It depends on how badly you mess up," she said.

"You Madisons and your cheeky jokes," Aiden said, chuckling.

"We make life more interesting," Nora answered.

"Yes, you do. And that's what I wanted to talk to you about," Aiden said, grateful for the opening. "What would you think of making this a permanent thing?"

"This what?" Nora asked.

"My office, you and me, you being here, here with me."

Nora was quiet for so long, he started to feel his stomach spin.

"It depends."

He reached for his napkin and dabbed at his face, trying to hide his panic. "On what?"

She folded her hands in her lap and studied him for a long moment. "Would my staying be as your nurse or as your wife?"

"My wife, of course." Aiden reached a hand toward her, and then pulled it away. "That is, if you want to be. I'd like you as my nurse too. Both? If you'd consider it?" Sweat broke out on his forehead.

"Are you asking me?" Nora asked, the hint of a smile on her lips and an eyebrow raised.

"I am." Aiden swallowed hard. "Nora, will you be my wife? I know I don't deserve someone as wonderful as you, but I'm in love with you. I want to spend the rest of my days with you by my side."

She picked up her fork and had a bite, and then took a maddeningly long time to answer. Finally, she tilted her head to the side, and said, "Yes, I accept."

Aiden mopped at his brow. "I was getting nervous. Are you going to do that to me often?"

Nora leaned close, the smile now wide on her face. She whispered, "Every day."

His own grin spread so wide his cheeks hurt. "I can't wait. I love you, Nora Madison."

Epilogue

A few months later

It was the most beautiful day for a church picnic. Nora's eyes roamed around at all the people there enjoying the potluck and the wonderful weather.

She spotted Gus talking with Mrs. Stover and her niece who had just moved to town to assist in the general store. Over to the side, Gavin was playing lively music on his violin, and children were clapping and dancing. Adults were watching, smiles on their faces.

Though there was still an undercurrent of sadness and loss for those who were no longer with them, the people of Red Ridge were slowly moving forward, leaning on each other in difficult moments, and helping each other to get through them.

Callie was sitting with Mirabelle, Winnie, and Hannah, and Nora worked her way toward them. They welcomed her with smiles and hugs. Nora squeezed Callie's hand gently before she let go, and prayed that the young woman would recover from her loss. She had so much more ahead of her, she was sure.

As she settled in with the women, Nora realized she'd never felt such a sense of belonging. Red Ridge had given her the things she'd needed most. A feeling of purpose, a sense of direction in her life.

The fact that it had also given her a beau was an added bonus. In a few months, wedding bells would be on the horizon for her. Until then, her days were spent helping Aiden in his office, spending time with her friends, and being part of the ladies' committee that had been busy helping those who needed them.

The sky darkened as clouds moved across the sun. Nora tipped her head up to watch, then squinted as the bright sun came back out. This was life, she thought. Moments of darkness before the light broke through.

In the distance, Billy caught her eye from where he stood talking with Eli and nodded, as if he knew what she was thinking. He probably did; they were so similar of a mind, they could have been twins.

"I'm sorry I'm late," Aiden said, as he came up to her. "Ladies," he greeted.

"No matter, I'm glad you are here," Nora said, happy when he sat next to her.

"I wouldn't miss the chance to spend more time with you for anything," Aiden said, his voice low. "You are the part of me I never knew was missing—until those moments we are separated."

Nora blushed, but smiled up at him. "I'm so in love with you," she whispered.

"Time for dessert!" Pastor Blackstone called out, startling her and Aiden from the kiss they were about to share.

"Aiden, come join us," Billy said and waved him over.

"Should I be worried?" Aiden asked the women. "He's been so friendly to me as of late. It's...disconcerting."

Hannah laughed. "You are one of them now."

"That's right," Winnie said. "You fought alongside them. That makes you a brother. You saved mine as well, and I'll forever be thankful."

Aiden looked at Nora slightly worriedly, but she squeezed his hand and then watched as he joined the gunslingers. Gavin put a hand on his shoulder, and soon the four—five when Nick joined—stood around laughing.

It was good to see, and Nora's heart felt light. She was looking forward to all that was ahead. One thing was for certain; with her brother and his friends around, life would always be interesting.

What's next?

Find out what happens when Callie tries to put the pieces of her life back together, and the gunslingers' friend Ryan Lundy visits Red Ridge, accidentally putting her in danger.

Book 5: The Tracker

https://www.amazon.com/Tracker-Red-Ridge-Chronicles-Book-ebook/dp/B0FGWKT2QM

***

And if you haven't already, be sure to get your FREE book in the Red Ridge Chronicles right here:

https://dl.bookfunnel.com/dt01yp1w38

Note from Author

Thank you for taking the time to read *The Doctor*.
Could I ask for one small favor? Reviews like yours on
Amazon mean so much to me and help others to find my
books! Even just a single line means a lot!

Also...

Want a FREE book?

Stop by my website to get your no strings attached **FREE
book**. It's my gift to you, as a thank you for reading this
one.

www.sarahlambbooks.com

Want a Free Red Ridge Chronicles Prequel?

Enjoy the gunslingers' adventure that happens just before Eli answers Hannah's ad.

The Riders

When an old friend calls, legendary gunslingers Eli Jones, Billy Madison, and Gavin Jefferson answer without hesitation. They've faced down the toughest outlaws, always bringing justice with deadly precision and no remorse. But nothing could prepare them for the fiery Stella, a woman determined to blaze her own trail—even at risk to one of their own.

As they race to prevent a catastrophe, the trio soon realizes that love is a more dangerous adversary than any outlaw.

These quick-draw, sharp-witted gunslingers have always sworn off settling down, but what happens next might just change their minds.

Discover the electrifying prequel to the Red Ridge Chronicles, a historical romance series in ebook, paperback, large print, and audiobook.

Read it in ebook here:

https://dl.bookfunnel.com/dt01yp1w38

Listen to it in audiobook here:

https://dl.bookfunnel.com/bq8tiktnwu

Read or Listen to the Red Ridge Chronicles Books

Amazon: https://www.amazon.com/dp/B0DQ7HFQ15

Audible:

https://www.audible.com/author/Sarah-Lamb/B098H3
SGLK

Book 1

The Gunslinger

Book 2

The Drifter

Book 3

The Lawman

Book 4

The Doctor

Book 5

The Tracker

Book 6

The Newcomer

Book 7

The Old Man

Book 8

The Christmas Rescue

About the Author

Sarah writes captivating characters and clean romance that's anything BUT boring! From heartbreaking moments to heartwarming tales, get swept away in either historical or small town romance that pulls you in until the last page.

Nestled in the Blue Ridge Mountains of Virginia where she's married to her Texan husband, you'll find Sarah creating her next book, homeschooling her two boys, or volunteering in her community.

Want more of Sarah's books? Find them all on Amazon!

https://www.amazon.com/stores/Sarah-Lamb/author/B098H3SGLK